Gordo and the
Hidden Treasure

The Woodland Frolics Series

Gordo
and the
Hidden
Treasure

By ADDA MAI SHARP

and EPSIE YOUNG
CO-ORDINATOR OF ELEMENTARY EDUCATION
AUSTIN PUBLIC SCHOOLS

ILLUSTRATED BY
ELIZABETH RICE

THE STECK COMPANY
PUBLISHERS • AUSTIN, TEXAS

Contents

Gordo and the
Hidden Treasure

CHAPTER 1 • Which Way to Treasure?

"Hidden treasure! Why can't we search for this hidden treasure tonight?" asked Gordo.

Four small masked faces were eagerly turned toward the old raccoon who stood guard over his little family in the September moonlight.

The young raccoons had been born in the hollow of an old oak tree early in May. Since then, the mother and father raccoon had searched far and wide over the plains and forests of northern Mexico for choice bits of food for their four babies.

For the last few weeks, the young raccoons had

9

gone hunting each night with their mother in the surrounding woodland. The little raccoons had listened in wide-eyed wonder as their mother had given them their first lessons in the art of hunting and of taking care of themselves.

She had taught them how to trail a mouse and how to catch a frog. She had taught them where to look for insects and how to find turtle eggs. She had taught them the look, the smell, the sound, and the feel of things about them.

The little raccoons now knew that a shadow across the moon could mean a hawk or an owl swooping down from the sky. They knew that a bark or a howl could mean loping coyotes or hunters' dogs on the run. They knew, too, that little peep-peeps meant baby birds in a nest, and little squeak-squeaks meant a field mouse was at home.

Tonight the little raccoons had returned from the longest trip they had ever made. The old raccoons had led them down to the river. There the little raccoons had learned how to wash a field mouse or a muddy frog in the swift water.

Here, tonight, at the foot of their den tree, the mother raccoon had told them that they now knew all the woodland trails. They would hunt together this fall and not go out of the woodland. Next year they could hunt alone and could go as far as they wished.

The father raccoon was always near by, ready to draw the attention of enemies to himself and away from his family. If the need should arise, he could put up a good fight with the fiercest creatures of the wilds. More than once he had whipped the dogs that hunters had set upon him. And more than once he had outwitted a cunning coyote.

Tonight the father raccoon was very proud of his half-grown offspring, who seemed to have learned their lessons so well.

"Next summer," he told them, "I shall take you on a treasure hunt. We shall go out of the woodland and beyond the village to search for a hidden golden treasure."

All the little raccoons were eager to start at once. They showed great disappointment when their father would not agree to go.

It was Gordo, the fat one, who was the most delighted with the idea of a treasure hunt. It was Gordo, the fat one, who begged the hardest to start at once. It was Gordo, the fat one, who dared

12

to ask, "Why can't we search for this hidden treasure tonight?"

"You are much too young to go looking for hidden treasure now," said the wise old raccoon. "And besides, look as you might, you could not find this golden treasure tonight. Run along, now! Up the tree! Up the tree and into your den! Perhaps at dawn your mother and I will bring home a good, fat chicken for you."

Up the tree to their old familiar hole went the four little raccoons. Gordo was the last to reach the hole. He watched his mother and father disappear into the shadows of the night. Then for some time he sat on a limb outside the hole and gazed into the woods flooded with moonlight.

Finally Gordo said to himself, "I am sure I could find the hidden treasure tonight. I think I could find it all by myself. I could go down the tree like this," he added, already backing his thick, bearlike body down the tree trunk. He held on carefully with his little black hands, which were as sensitive and nimble as human hands.

"There now! That was easy!" he said as he
reached the ground. "Now I wonder which way
leads to the hidden treasure."

Gordo was only half-grown, but he was a strong
little fellow. Although he seemed clumsy and lazy,
he was not lacking in courage; and he had more
than his share of curiosity.

Gordo was about twenty-four inches long and already weighed nearly twenty pounds. As the Spanish name, Gordo, indicates, he was a fat fellow. There was nothing Gordo liked better than food, and there was nothing he liked less than work!

Gordo's brownish black and gray fur was thick and glossy. The marking around his eyes gave him the appearance of wearing a black mask. His long, bushy, black-ringed tail was something to be proud of.

Gordo now stood at the foot of the den tree and looked all around. The woodland seemed big and lonesome. Already the yellow moon was sinking low, leaving dark shadows everywhere.

"Which way? If I only knew which way to go," Gordo muttered.

"Why don't you ask me? I know all the trails around here," said a voice behind Gordo.

Gordo looked around quickly. There, clinging head downward on the tree trunk, was his old friend and neighbor, Rojo, the red squirrel.

"Oh, Rojo!" said Gordo. "I am starting on a treasure hunt. There is a rich golden treasure hidden somewhere around here. I am sure that it is good to eat. When I find it, what a feast I shall have! Which way should I go to find it?"

Rojo chattered and scolded, "I think you should not go at all, Gordo. You cannot run fast. You cannot travel far. You don't know the tricks of your enemies. And—you don't even know which way to start! Sometimes the richest treasure is right under your nose, if you will only wait and watch for it."

"Oh, but this is a hidden treasure!" replied Gordo. "And I don't think you know which way to go, either, Rojo."

16

"No, I do not know where your golden treasure is hidden," said Rojo. "The only hidden treasure I know about is the treasure of nuts and acorns that I have hidden for use in the winter. I have heard, however, that rare treasures are hidden in many parts of Mexico."

Rojo scampered down to the ground and looked closely at the fat, adventurous little raccoon. With a twinkle in his big bright eyes, Rojo said, "If you are sure you want to go on this treasure hunt, I'll show you the way out of the woods."

"Let's go!" said Gordo, and soon the swift red squirrel and the shuffling little raccoon were on their way.

CHAPTER 2 • The First Treasure Hunt

Gordo and Rojo traveled along happily. They looked here and there for insects. They climbed trees to look for birds' eggs. Finally, Rojo led Gordo to a wild grapevine, loaded with ripe purple grapes.

While the two little creatures were eating the juicy ripe grapes, Rojo asked, "Do you know who went on the first treasure hunt on earth?"

"No," replied Gordo. "Who was it? What did he seek?"

"It was a squirrel," said Rojo. "In fact, three brown squirrels went to seek a treasure of fire from the sky. Let me tell you the legend of the first treasure hunt and the earth's first fire. My grandfather told the legend to me, and he had heard it told over and over by the Indians."

"Good! I like to hear Indian legends," cried Gordo.

There, in the early morning darkness that comes just before the dawn, Rojo told this story:

"Long, long ago, people called Aztecs lived in Mexico. The Aztecs worshiped the sun because it gave warmth to their bodies and made their fruits and grains grow.

"But long before the time of the Aztecs, the animals ruled the land. The animals, too, looked to the sun for warmth and comfort. As long as the great fireball of the heavens was shining, the animals were happy.

"There came a time, however, when dark clouds blotted out the sun. For days and days the rain poured down, and the sky was dark and cold.

"Since there was no fire upon the earth, the poor animals had no way to dry their wet skins and warm their chilled bodies.

"The king of the beasts finally called all the animals together. He told them that they must seek the treasure of fire, and he asked for volunteers.

"Three gay young squirrels volunteered to go up to the sky and seek a flaming torch from the great fireball. As the other animals watched, the three brown squirrels raced up the tallest tree, higher, higher, higher, until at last they disappeared into the great blue sky.

"After searching for a long time, the squirrels found the precious fire treasure hidden behind a big, dark cloud. Each brown squirrel took a flaming torch to carry down to the earth.

"The first squirrel was afraid of the flames and blew them out. When he reached the earth, he found that the smoldering torch had covered his fur with a coat of gray smoke and ashes. And to this day, all his grandchildren are gray."

21

"What about the other two squirrels?" asked Gordo, as he lightly brushed his own heavy gray fur.

"Well," said Rojo, "the second brown squirrel was not afraid of the flames, but he was very selfish. He decided to keep the torch for himself and use it to frighten away his enemies. He hid the torch in his deep fur, hoping that the animals would think he had lost it on his way down from the sky.

"But when he reached the earth, he found that the torch had burned his fur until it was black instead of brown. And to this day, his grandchildren are all black from head to foot."

"Black squirrels!" exclaimed Gordo. "And what

about the third squirrel who went to seek the fire treasure for the earth?"

"The third brown squirrel was my great-great-grandfather," Rojo said proudly. "He was a brave little fellow who really wanted to help the creatures on the earth. He hurried down from the sky, taking great care that his torch would not be blown out by the wind. When he reached the earth, he gave the torch to the king of the animals.

"The king soon started a great fire—the first fire on earth. All of the cold, wet creatures danced in its warmth and were happy again.

"The king thanked the little brown squirrel for being so brave and so kind. Then he blew the beautiful golden-red glow of the fire onto the squirrel's soft, furry breast as a mark of his great courage.

"And, to this day, Great-great-grandfather Rojo's grandchildren all wear a golden-red coat! See!"

CHAPTER 3 • The Devil in the Bell Tower

"Listen! I hear singing," said Gordo, after Rojo had finished his story.

"You hear ringing," replied Rojo. "That is a church bell ringing in the village."

"Oh, I have never heard a bell before! And I have never seen a village!" exclaimed Gordo.

"You will hear many bells and see many villages if you search for a hidden treasure in Mexico," replied Rojo. "That church bell is ringing for an early service. It means that daylight will come quickly now. And that means that you should go home and sleep all through the day."

25

"Oh, no," said Gordo, "I am now on my way and will not turn back. I see a deserted hawk's nest in the top of this tree. It will make a good sunny bed for me when daylight comes."

Before saying good-by to Gordo, Rojo warned him of dogs, foxes, and coyotes; of swooping eagles and stealthy pumas; and of the fierce wild peccaries called javelinas. Then, with a flick of his tail and a hop, skip, and jump, Rojo was gone.

Gordo was alone for the first time in his life. He was a little excited but not really afraid, for Gordo was a brave little fellow.

He tried to recall all the things that his mother had taught him on those happy walks through the woods. He recalled the pleasant sound of a frog's leap into the water and the welcome drumming of insects in rotten logs. He knew that his teeth were sharp and strong. He knew that his front feet were more than just feet to walk on—they were real little hands with fingers so nimble and sensitive that they seemed to have eyes in their tips. He knew that he was too big for the horned owl

to catch, and he thought that he was too clever
to be caught by any of his other enemies.

Like all raccoons, Gordo had his full share of
curiosity. Right now this curiosity centered on
the church bell ringing in the village.

Gordo looked at the dark sky. He cast a glance
at the black lump in the treetop—his hawk's-nest
bed. Then he started slowly down the tree.

27

"I'll have a look at that ringing, singing bell before I curl up for my day's nap," he said. "And
who knows? The golden treasure may be hidden
there!"

When Gordo walked out of his woodland, he
found an entirely different world. Big cactus
plants stood stiffly on the plains, and there were
but few trees to climb in case of danger.

Gordo shuffled along without stopping to explore the new country. As he approached the village, he saw many small houses with brightly colored tile roofs.

Gordo grunted and raised the fur on his back as he turned a corner and found himself face to face with a great, dark beast. But the great, dark beast proved to be only a small, sleepy burro.

As he traveled on, Gordo came at last to the church with the singing bell. Below the bell tower stood a man, pulling a rope back and forth.

"Here it is!" exclaimed Gordo. "But how can I see the singing bell? I do not dare go in while the man is there."

Then Gordo heard another bell ringing and hurried toward the sound. But at that church another man was pulling a rope back and forth.

"Oh, my! Now where shall I go?" thought Gordo.

Since Gordo was not the kind of fellow who would give up easily, he ran on down the street and found still another church. This time no one was in sight.

Gordo climbed up to a window and peeped inside.

"Golden treasure!" he exclaimed as he saw the candlesticks and decorations in the little church. "But these are not hidden! Anyone can see them. They are not the hidden golden treasure that I am seeking."

Gordo then went to the bell tower and looked all around. Finally he looked up. Hanging there in the shadows was a great, dark bell with a rope swinging down from it.

31

"A bell! A singing bell!" cried Gordo. "But why is it not singing as the other bells are? Perhaps if I should pull the rope, it would sing; but I cannot reach the rope. Perhaps if I climb the tower, I can make it sing." At once he began climbing into the bell tower—up and up and up!

While Gordo was making his way to the top of the bell tower, Pedro was hurrying as fast as he could toward the church. Pedro was the man who was paid to ring the bell each morning. Today Pedro was late. The other church bells were ringing merrily, but Pedro's bell was silent and still.

32

Pedro had left home on time that morning. In the plaza he had seen the old trader who sold sweet cakes to the people who came to early service. The old man, with his blanket wrapped around him and his basket of sweet cakes beside him, was sound asleep.

"How good a sweet cake would taste in this cool hour of dawn!" thought Pedro.

The farther Pedro walked, the more he wanted a sweet cake. But Pedro had no money with him.

"The old trader would never miss just one sweet cake, since he has a whole basketful," thought Pedro. "I will go back to the plaza and take one— just one—sweet cake from the sleeping trader's basket."

After taking the sweet cake, Pedro hurried to the church and rushed to the bell tower. He pulled the rope stoutly, but a strange sound came from the bell: "Bog! Bog!"

"There is no music in the bell!" cried Pedro.

Again and again Pedro pulled the rope. Again

and again there was no gay ringing in the bell—
only the flat, dead sound, "Bog! Bog!"

Pedro was afraid now. He exclaimed, "Why
will not my good bell ring? Is it not the finest bell
in the town? Did it not come all the way from
Mexico City—or was it even from faraway Spain?"

Pedro thought about his being late for his task.
He thought about his taking the sweet cake from
the poor old sleeping trader. Then he took his
flashlight and threw the spot of light high into the
tower and onto the bell. There in the shadows he
saw something clinging to the swaying bell. He
looked again and saw a small face in a black mask.

35

"Oh, it is the devil himself!" cried Pedro, and he rushed headlong out of the bell tower and went screaming down the street.

"The devil is in the bell tower! Get him out! Get him out!" he cried. "I am sorry I took the sweet cake! I will pay the trader for the sweet cake! Only send this masked devil away and let my good bell ring again!"

While the people rushed to Pedro's side, Gordo reached the bell rope and let himself down, hand over hand.

"Dong!" went the bell as the rope swayed to one side. "Dong!" it went again as the rope and the raccoon swayed to the other side.

"Listen! The devil is tolling my bell!" cried Pedro to the crowd around him.

Gordo heard all the noise, and he was frightened. He hurried as much as a fat raccoon can hurry and dropped to the ground, running as he landed.

By the time the people with their sticks and stones reached the bell tower, Gordo was well on his way out of the village. He did not stop until he reached the safety of the woodland. He climbed the tree hurriedly and was soon curled up in the deserted hawk's nest for a good long sleep in the sunshine.

CHAPTER 4 · El Capitán

Gordo turned and stretched and yawned after his daylong sleep in the treetop.

"Where on earth am I?" he thought as he heard a crunching sound far beneath him.

He crawled out on a limb and looked down through the branches. On the ground he saw a queer little animal eating acorns.

"Could that be El Capitán, the old javelina?" Gordo wondered to himself. "Rojo told me to take no chances with those peccaries, and Mother said El Capitán is the fiercest javelina in these woods!"

39

Gordo was wide awake now and realized where he was. He realized, too, that the woods around him were quite shadowy. Then he heard bells ringing in the village.

"Can those bells still be ringing!" he said aloud to himself.

"Not still, but again," said a voice below him.

Gordo then saw a stranger on the limb beneath him. The creature looked a little like Gordo. It had grayish-brown fur and a long, bushy tail that was ringed with light bands. This animal was not as fat as Gordo, and its eyes and ears seemed too big for its small, catlike face.

"Who are you?" asked Gordo.

"I am Ringo, the ring-tailed cat," replied the stranger. "I know you, Gordo, but I do not know what you are doing so far from your den tree, and all alone. I am a cousin of the raccoon family, and I know where you live."

"Oh!" said Gordo. "Are you my cousin? Perhaps you will go with me to search for the hidden treasure."

40

The ring-tailed cat drew himself up tall and said in a surprised voice, "Hidden treasure! No, I don't want to search for hidden treasure! I have heard that rich treasures are hidden near the great pyramids—the Pyramid of the Sun and the Pyramid of the Moon. One must cross the desert to get to the pyramids, though, and all kinds of dangers lie in the desert!"

"The Pyramid of the Sun and the Pyramid of the Moon!" Gordo exclaimed. "Father spoke of a golden treasure. Golden is the sunlight, and golden is the autumn moon. That must be where the golden treasure is hidden!"

"Hear the evening bells ringing," said the ring-tailed cat. "That means that it is sundown. Now we may safely look for supper."

As the two little animals jumped to the ground, an old javelina came running and snarling. The little raccoon and the ring-tailed cat had to scamper back up the tree.

"You can't take a chance with El Capitán," Ringo warned. "He is the oldest and the fiercest javelina in this country. And he leads his band of wild peccaries like a captain leads an army. That is why we call him El Capitán."

Gordo had his first close look at the little animal with its stiff white collar. The javelina was about three feet long and two feet high. He liked to eat as well as Gordo did and would eat nuts, roots, fruits, frogs, and almost anything else.

42

"My! El Capitán eats like a pig," said Gordo.

"Yes, he does eat like a pig. He is a kind of wild pig," replied the ring-tailed cat.

"I like his stiff white collar, but I do not like his long, sharp teeth!" said Gordo.

"Be still! Someone is coming!" warned Ringo.

Gordo looked and whispered, "It's a dog—no, two big gray dogs!"

"Not dogs—coyotes!" replied Ringo. "You always have to look out for coyotes when you are on the ground!"

El Capitán stood very still and looked at the two big coyotes. One coyote stood at his right side, and the other stood at his left side. El Capitán knew that there was no chance of his getting away.

He knew that the coyotes were very smart animals. He knew, too, that he must prove that he was as smart as they were or be eaten by them.

"Hello, Mr. Coyote!" said the old javelina.

"Hello, Mr. Javelina!" said the coyote.

"Will you have some of these good acorns?"
asked El Capitán.

Mr. Coyote shook his head and said, "I don't
think acorns would be very good for coyotes.
What do you think, Mrs. Coyote?"

"Oh, no! I do not think acorns would be very good for coyotes," agreed Mrs. Coyote.

Mr. Coyote licked his mouth and said, "Now, peccary meat would be very good for coyotes."

"Oh, yes! Peccary meat would be very good for coyotes," agreed Mrs. Coyote.

The coyotes moved a little closer to El Capitán. Then Mr. Coyote said, "Mr. Javelina, we are going to eat you right now!"

El Capitán knew that he must think fast. He raised his tiny ears and wiggled his funny little nose. Then he said, "I am such an old javelina! One little old javelina like me will not be enough for two big, fine coyotes like you! I have a fat brother just over the hill. If you will not eat me right now, I shall call him."

"A fat peccary would be better. What do you think, Mrs. Coyote?" said Mr. Coyote.

"Oh, yes, a fat peccary would be much better," agreed Mrs. Coyote. "Then we could each have one!" she whispered to Mr. Coyote.

"Call your fat brother," said Mr. Coyote.

El Capitán gave a little squeal, and over the hill came a fat peccary.

Mr. Coyote licked his mouth. Mrs. Coyote licked her mouth. But El Capitán cried, "Oh, the wrong brother came! I have a brother much bigger and fatter than this one!"

"Then call your other brother," said Mr. Coyote, and he whispered to Mrs. Coyote, "Now we shall have three peccaries!"

El Capitán squealed, and a big fat peccary came over the hill. El Capitán could hear Mr. Coyote's fast breathing. He could hear Mrs. Coyote's fast breathing and could see her red tongue between her long teeth.

Mrs. Coyote looked at Mr. Coyote and said, "One for you and one for me and one for our four baby coyotes!"

"Four baby coyotes!" exclaimed El Capitán. "My two brothers and I will not be enough for all of you! I have three little brothers over the hill. If you will not eat us right now, I shall call them, too. Then you will have one peccary for each baby coyote and one for each of you."

"I don't know about that," said Mr. Coyote.

"Oh, yes!" said Mrs. Coyote. "Then we would not have to hunt any tomorrow."

"Very well, call your three little brothers," agreed Mr. Coyote.

El Capitán laughed to himself. The fat brother and the big fat brother laughed a little, too. Then El Capitán raised his head and squealed and squealed and squealed!

Over the hill came a peccary.

"Oh," laughed Mrs. Coyote, "Mr. Javelina is very foolish! Soon we shall kill him and all his brothers, too!"

Over the hill came another peccary.

"Oh," said Mr. Coyote, "this will be fun!"

Over the hill came another peccary.

"One, two, three," said Mrs. Coyote. "Now there is one for each of us!"

But—over the hill came another peccary!
"Look, still another!" said Mrs. Coyote.
Over the hill came another peccary—and

another, and another, and another! On and on they came like marching soldiers. Their stiff hair was standing straight up, and their long white teeth were shining.

The two coyotes were so surprised that they could not move! They kept watching for the last peccary to come over the hill, but there was always another and still another. At last Mr. and Mrs. Coyote were completely surrounded by peccaries.

The two coyotes began to huff and puff and snap their teeth. But the peccaries came on and on.

"We must run like the wind!" cried Mr. Coyote to Mrs. Coyote. And run they did, while the peccaries nipped and slashed at their sides.

When the coyotes were out of sight, El Capitán and his soldiers marched back over the hill to nibble roots and fruits and anything else they could find.

CHAPTER 5 · The Galloping Ghost

When the greedy coyotes and the fierce javelinas had gone, Gordo and Ringo came down from
the tree. Since they were hungry, they set out at
once to find something to eat.

"Come this way! We shall find more food in the
village," said Ringo.

"I do not like the village. The people there
make too much noise! I'll take this road to the
left," said Gordo.

"Follow that road and you'll land in the desert! What do you think you can find in the desert?" asked the ring-tailed cat.

"I may find the hidden treasure there," replied Gordo.

"You may find yourself pricked to pieces or skinned alive!" Ringo cried. "The desert is full of ghosts and goblins!" He waved good-by to the fat raccoon and went on his way toward the village.

Gordo caught a grasshopper in midair. Later he found eggs in a groundbird's nest. With food in his stomach, he started down the road that led to the desert.

The farther Gordo went, the fewer trees he saw. At first there were only lacy mesquites. Farther on, he found that these trees gave up their places in the sand and on the rocky hillsides to dwarf growths of creosote bushes, yuccas, and cactus plants.

When the moon came up, Gordo found himself in the midst of this desert wonderland. There was a kind of enchantment about the desert with its spiny vegetation. There was also a great deal for a curious raccoon to investigate.

Gordo was fascinated by the weird forms around him. He thought it looked like a good place for hidden treasure, too.

"Cactus, cactus, cactus!" he said as he looked at first one plant and then another. "Yum, yum," he added as he noticed the plump red-gold fruit on the thick prickly pear beside him. "These look good!"

A moment later the little raccoon groaned and cried with pain. The great needles of the cactus had pricked his hands and stung his nose!

"I'll not bother those cactus fruits again!" Gordo cried. "They are probably sour anyway. I'll look for a field mouse, instead."

As Gordo hunted for field mice among the desert growth, he heard something moving in the sand. He reached out his little black hand and seized it. But as he felt the creature, Gordo dropped it and drew back in surprise.

"Is everything in the desert thorny?" he exclaimed as he gazed at the little animal he had dropped.

Gordo had picked up a small horned lizard which is usually called a horned toad. Like all horned toads, this little fellow's spotted skin was covered with tiny spikes, or horns.

"Ghosts and goblins! You must be a goblin! Or are you a little dragon?" Gordo asked.

The small horned toad flattened his pale sand-colored body against the sand until he could hardly be seen. After a moment's time, he raised his chest high and wagged his horny head from side to side.

"I am not a goblin, and I am not a dragon!" he said. "You don't see me breathing fire, do you?"

"No," replied Gordo, "but I did see you shoot blood out of your eye!"

Just then Gordo heard someone laughing above his head, "Cha-cha! Cha-cha, cha-cha!"

He looked up but could see no one. He turned to ask the horned toad who it was that was laughing. But the little toad had completely buried himself in the sand and had disappeared as if by magic.

Again Gordo heard the laugh, "Cha-cha, cha-cha!" This time he looked high into the giant cactus beside him. There he saw the creature that was laughing at him. Its tiny face peeped at Gordo from a small hole in the body of the big cactus stalk.

"Well, well! Who are you?" asked Gordo.

"I am an elf," said the little creature.

"An elf? So the desert has elves as well as goblins and ghosts!" said Gordo.

"Yes, I am an elf owl," said the tiny bird as it flew out of its hole and back again.

Gordo saw that the little bird was indeed an elf owl, the tiniest owl in the world. It was just about the size of a redbird.

"How did you ever make a hole in that thorny cactus?" Gordo asked.

"I didn't," replied the elf owl. "The wood-peckers make holes in the cactus plants. When they leave them, we take them for our homes. And very safe homes they are, too."

The elf owl turned his head right and left. He looked up and he looked down. "I hear a voice," he said, and he dropped into the hole and out of sight.

Gordo thought he heard a voice, too. Making his way carefully among the thorny desert plants, he stopped at last by a creosote bush from which the voice seemed to come.

"I'll eat you and put the next one in my pocket," said the voice.

The hair stood up on Gordo's back. He stood very still and looked all around. No one was in sight.

"I'll eat you and put the next one in my pocket," said the voice.

"There it is again! A voice without a body! It must be a ghost!" thought Gordo.

57

Then Gordo heard a slight rustle in the stiff desert grass at the foot of the creosote bush. He saw a pale tuft of hair swish in the brown grass. In a flash he held a frightened little animal in his small black hands.

Gordo was very happy about catching this animal, for it looked a little like a big field mouse. Its sand-colored fur was fine and silky. Even its feet were furred so that it could travel silently over the sand. Its seven-inch tail, which was several inches longer than its body, had a bushy tuft at the tip. Its forelegs were small and short; but its hind legs, like those of a kangaroo, were both strong and long. Because of its long hind legs, the little animal is called a kangaroo rat.

"You are a funny fellow!" Gordo exclaimed. "Tell me, how did you think you could eat me or put me in your pocket?"

The shy little animal flattened his small round ears against his big head. He blinked his shoe-button eyes and wiggled his long whiskers. Then in a squeaky little voice he said, "Oh, I didn't mean to eat you or to put you in my pocket! I am only a galloping ghost of the desert, and I eat nothing but seeds! I was talking to a head of grass seed that I had found."

"A galloping ghost!" exclaimed Gordo. "Well, tell me, Mr. Galloping Ghost, where are your pockets?"

"Here at the sides of my cheeks. And they are fur-lined, too," replied the kangaroo rat as he put his paws on the openings of the pouches beside his nose.

"So you carry the seeds home in your pockets, do you?" said Gordo, who had no handy pockets for his food.

"Yes, I carry them to my underground home to eat in the winter," said the trembling little fellow.

"How do you empty those pockets?" asked Gordo.

60

"Like this," said the kangaroo rat, as he pressed at the back of his pockets with his paws. Out popped a teaspoonful of seed from each furry pocket!

Gordo gazed in wonder at the furry pockets. Then he said to the galloping ghost, "Well, I don't have any pockets, but I am hungry. I'll just wash you and eat you!"

61

"Oh, please don't put me in the water!" begged the little desert ghost. "I don't like water! I never drink water, and I take my bath in the sand! Please don't put me in the water!"

"I always wash my meat before I eat it," replied Gordo. "Where is the stream?"

"There is no stream in the desert. Only sand and cactus are here," said the kangaroo rat.

"Then where do the desert creatures get water?" asked Gordo.

"Those who drink water must get it from the desert water barrels," said the little desert ghost.

"Desert water barrels?" asked Gordo.

"Yes, the Indians cut the tops off some of the barrel cactus plants. Then the sap from the plant fills the barrel with sweet, fresh water," the kangaroo rat explained.

"I am glad to know about these desert water barrels," said Gordo. "Here is a big water barrel. Now I can wash you and eat you."

When Gordo touched the cactus, hundreds of needles pricked his flesh, just as the kangaroo rat had known they would do. Crying out with pain, Gordo dropped the little animal on the sand.

That was all the galloping ghost wanted. With one great leap he landed fifteen feet away from the fat raccoon. Then, with his long tail as a rudder, he went galloping across the sand like a wisp of gray smoke.

CHAPTER 6 • Secondhand Treasure

"Another desert ghost!" said Gordo as he looked at a huge cactus that the wind had blown down. It lay like a sprawling giant on the sand.

Suddenly Gordo saw two big ears move behind the fallen giant. Since he thought the ears might belong to a coyote, he began to wonder where he could hide. Before he could steal away, out jumped Mr. Jeep, the oldest and wisest jack rabbit in the country.

65

"Gordo!" exclaimed Mr. Jeep. "What in the world are you doing in the desert?"

"I am about to starve to death—that's what I'm doing!" replied Gordo.

"These cactus apples are very delicious," said Mr. Jeep. "Many have fallen off the plant; so you won't get pricked as you reach for them. Why don't you try them?"

"These are really delicious!" said Gordo, as he cautiously tasted the purple-red fruits, shaped like fat little cucumbers.

The fully ripe fruits had burst open, showing their bright red pulp and hundreds of tiny black seeds.

"We were lucky to find this fallen plant before the Indians came to harvest the fruits," said Mr. Jeep.

"Do the Indians really use the cactus apples?" asked Gordo.

"Oh, yes," replied Mr. Jeep. "The Indians separate the seeds and the juice from the pulp. They use the pulp for jam, and they grind the seeds into a rich, oily mush. They boil the juice down to a syrup and keep it to use in the winter."

"Well, the Indians may like the desert, but I have not found it so good for raccoons," said Gordo.

"The Indians call it a friendly desert," Mr. Jeep continued. "They make fences from the organpipe cactus. They make candles from a waxlike resin found in one kind of cactus. They find sweet water in the barrel cactus, and they sometimes use this cactus for a cooking pot by dropping hot stones into it. They enjoy the tasty fruits of many kinds of cactus plants. They make dye and glue and medicine from the long, twisted seed pods of the mesquite tree and from the bitter sap of the creosote bush. They use cactus fibres to make ropes, to weave baskets, and even to cover their roofs."

"I didn't know that the desert was so friendly to the Indians," said Gordo.

Mr. Jeep winked at Gordo and added, "Sometimes they even catch a foolish jack rabbit or a fat raccoon who has eaten so much he cannot run away!"

"Oh, Mr. Jeep! You are so very wise!" laughed Gordo. "Perhaps you can tell me whether any treasure is hidden in this desert. You see, I am seeking a hidden treasure!"

"Um-m-m! So you are seeking a hidden treasure!" said Mr. Jeep. "Well, I don't think you will find it here. I have heard that the great king of the Aztecs hid his people's gold here at the foot of a creosote bush when Mexico was invaded by the Spaniards. But the ground squirrels, the gophers, and the galloping ghosts have dug up every foot of this desert and have never found the treasure. If any treasure is hidden in the desert, it must be in the store of the desert's secondhand trader."

"Secondhand trader! Is there a secondhand store in the desert?" asked Gordo. Before Mr. Jeep could answer, Gordo added, "Do you know where this secondhand store is?"

"Do I know where this secondhand store is? Of

68

course, Mr. Question-box," replied the old jack rabbit. "I know where the tarantula holes are! I know where the collared lizards make tracks! I know where the horned toad sleeps! I know where the rattlesnakes hide! I know which cactus is home for the elf owl! I know where the white-winged dove has her nest! I know where the red-tailed hawk seeks his food! I know all the tunnels of the galloping ghost! I know the tricks of the coyote and the mink! And you ask me if I know where the secondhand store of the desert is! Come with me!"

Off across the desert went the rabbit and the raccoon, each leaving his own peculiar footprints in the sand. Mr. Jeep's tracks were small and oddly grouped. Gordo's tracks looked almost like a baby's footprints.

Soon Mr. Jeep stopped beside a big prickly pear. On the ground around the plant was a huge pile of spiny cactus joints, sticks, twigs, and chips. The pile was nearly five feet high.

"What is all this?" asked Gordo.

69

"This," said Mr. Jeep, "is the home and the second-hand store of Mr. White-throat, the wood rat— or pack rat or trade rat, as some call him."

"Oh, dear me!" exclaimed Gordo. "How can anyone get inside this secondhand store?"

"Well, Mr. White-throat gets in and out, and he always carries something with him as he comes and as he goes! You, too, can find a way to get inside if you work hard enough! Good-by and good luck!" said Mr. Jeep. And away he ran, in and out among the thorny desert plants.

Gordo pushed and pulled and finally made his way into the wood rat's home and store. Mr. White-throat was out trading some of his goods; so Gordo had the place to himself. Once inside the nest, Gordo had a good time examining all the secondhand treasures.

71

"I wonder where he found all these things and what he left in exchange for the ones he took!" exclaimed Gordo as he picked up one thing after another.

He picked up nails, twigs, tin cans, spoons, papers, a match cover, a half dollar, a potato, and many, many other things. Then his eyes fell upon a gleaming golden object beneath a lot of trash. Gordo pulled the round golden object out and examined it carefully.

"Oh, my," he cried, "this is a golden treasure! Perhaps it is the treasure that I am seeking! It has a long golden tail! And it must be alive, for I can hear its heart beat, 'tick, tick'!"

Gordo picked his prickly way out of the second-hand store and started across the desert. Mr. Jeep had told him of some dripping springs on the far edge of the desert. It was to these springs that Gordo hastened.

"I'll wash this thing and eat it if it is as good as I hope it is!" he said as he ran along.

It was nearly dawn when Gordo reached the springs and heard the welcome sound of the water dripping over the rocks. He was surprised to find that a Mexican man, with his burro train, had camped for the night beside the rocky springs. Now, in the first shadowy light of the day, the man

was getting his ten pack burros ready for the day's trip.

Gordo crept by the burros and went at once to wash his new-found treasure in the water. He swished it back and forth in the spring and then tried to bite it. It was too hard; so he held it in the water again.

"So you are the thief who took my watch from my pocket while I slept and put a chip in its place!" exclaimed the man as he caught sight of Gordo and the golden treasure.

The man was rushing toward Gordo. He had a long whip in his hand. This was too much for the little raccoon. He dropped the watch and chain on the ground and darted out among the burros to hide.

One burro seemed more friendly than the others. He even rubbed Gordo with his nose. This burro was carrying two big baskets, one at each of his sides. Gordo leaped upon the friendly burro's back and dropped out of sight into the empty basket.

74

The man picked up his watch and looked for the fat raccoon, but he could not find him. Then he called, "Arre, burro!" The burros knew that this meant, "Get up!" and soon they were plodding down the road.

Gordo did not know where he was going. He did know that daylight had come and that the desert sun would be very hot. He was glad that he had found the nice basket in which he could sleep until the friendly evening shadows would come again.

As he curled himself into a furry ball at the bottom of the basket, he said to himself, "That was only a secondhand treasure, and besides, it was not good to eat!"

CHAPTER 7 · Ventriloquist of the Woods

After a long time Gordo was awakened by the clippity-clop of hoofs on the cobblestones as the burros jogged along a village street. He looked out of his basket bed and saw that the village streets were quite dark. The only timepiece Gordo had, his stomach, told him that it was suppertime.

At the edge of the village the man stopped his burros and began to prepare his camp for the night. Gordo said good-by to the friendly little burro who had carried him far away from the desert. Then he made his way safely into the nearby woodland before the man could catch sight of him.

77

Soon Gordo came to a lazy little tropical river with water as green as the ocean. It moved slowly along as if it did not want to leave the moss-draped trees that cast their shadows upon it. The banks of such a river made a fine picnic ground for a raccoon. Here a raccoon could find plenty of food without having to work for it.

Gordo robbed a bird's nest of its eggs; he dug a frog out of the mud; he waded in the shallow water near the river bank and plucked out mussels and even slapped a few fresh-water fish out of the stream.

When he had filled his stomach, he wandered farther into the woods. He soon discovered that the woodland reached far up the side of a mountain. As Gordo waddled along, he heard many sounds that were strange to him. He had never been in the mountains and had never traveled through such jungle growth before.

Suddenly there was such a noise of "cheeps" and "chocks" that Gordo crouched behind a big cypress tree to see who was making such a noise. He did

78

not have to wait long, for the noisemakers settled in the top of the cypress tree.

Gordo could then see that these great clacking birds were only a flock of long-tailed grackles. For some time he watched them show off by stretching their bills upward and their tails downward and by fluffing out their feathers and spreading wide their big tails.

"Hello, Mr. Grackle!" called Gordo.

The big grackles let out such a clatter of "cheeps" and "chocks" that Gordo was almost sorry he had spoken. When they were quiet again, he said, "I am seeking a hidden treasure and—"

"Yes, our eggs, no doubt!" interrupted a big shiny grackle, with his bill in the air.

"Oh, no! I am seeking a golden treasure," said Gordo. "I thought you might tell me where to look for it!"

The big birds looked at each other and chuckled. Then Mr. Grackle, the leader of the flock, replied, "Mr. Raccoon, there is no hidden treasure of gold in these woods. If you will go over the top of the mountain, and down again, you will come to the wild pineapple thickets. You might find something there!"

Gordo was glad to leave the noisy grackles, but he did not find the trip to the top of the mountain an easy one. He met strange creatures and heard strange voices. He longed for the banks of the quiet tropical river, and sometimes he wished he had never started looking for the hidden treasure.

81

Green and gold macaws flew in and out among the trees. A queer little screech owl, with ear tufts raised and eyes half-closed, watched Gordo pass beneath its tree. An armadillo that had come out to look for food flattened its armored body against the ground as Gordo approached. A chubby little honey bear plucked a plum from a tree with its monkey-like tail and licked the pulp from the seed with its long, rough tongue. A flock of red-crowned parrots chattered endlessly as they feasted on the blossoms of a tropical tree. A white-tailed doe stood with one foot raised as Gordo came close to the bed of her spotted fawn.

"What are you looking for?" the doe asked.

"I am looking for hidden treasure—golden hidden treasure," Gordo replied.

"There is no hidden golden treasure here," said the doe.

"Mr. Grackle said there might be treasure hidden in the wild pineapple thicket. That is where I have started," said Gordo.

"Oh, that Mr. Grackle! He is a great joker," said the doe. "There is no treasure in the pineapple thicket, Gordo. Don't go there! You will be torn to pieces! The sharp, spiny thorns of the wild pineapple plants will slash your skin like a thousand knives! And besides a spotted jaguar and her pretty kittens come out of the woods and hunt near the wild pineapple thickets. Who knows! You might be just what she would like to have for her kittens' supper! Don't go there, Gordo!"

Gordo was afraid now. His fur rose on his back as he thought of the big, spotted jaguar. He looked all around. When he turned to thank the kind little doe, she and her fawn had disappeared.

As Gordo stood very still and wondered which way he should go, he heard a strange call on the air, "Oompa, oompa, oompa!"

After a moment, Gordo started toward the sound, which he thought came from the top of a nearby tree. Before he had gone three steps, there it was again, "Oompa, oompa!" This time the sound seemed to come from the tree right over his head.

"I'll go up there and find that 'oompa,'" thought Gordo, and up he went. When he reached the top of the tree, he found only an old rusty lizard. It scuttled out of the reach of Gordo's swift fingers.

"Oompa, oompa!" There it was again. This time it sounded miles away!

85

Gordo was about to start down the tree when a big bird lighted on the limb beside him. Gordo looked at the gray-brown bird and asked, "Did you make that funny 'oompa' sound?"

"Oh, no, I am Papán. See!" said the big Mexican jay. And he began to bob his tail up and down and scream.

Papán is a strange, brownish Mexican jay who has a queer little bag on his chest. When he screams, the bag fills with air and then collapses suddenly with a sharp explosive sound.

"Oh, I see!" said Gordo, laughing. "You do not say 'oompa,' but you say 'Papán,' as if you had the hiccups!"

86

"Yes, that is how I got my name—Papán, the sound of a hiccup!" replied the funny jay.

"Oompa, oompa!" There it was again, but now it seemed to be on the ground beneath Gordo and Papán.

"That is the curassow that you hear. He is the ventriloquist of the woods," said Papán.

Then Papán showed Gordo the big black and white curassow. He was hiding among the leaves of their tree, not three feet from where they were sitting.

"Ventriloquist of the woods!" exclaimed Gordo. "Well, Mr. Ventriloquist, did you make all those 'oompas' I heard? And were you sitting right here in this tree all the time?"

"That is right, Mr. Raccoon. I am a ventriloquist, and I can put my 'oompa' anywhere I want it!" replied the big curassow.

The solemn booming began again. First it seemed to come from high up on the mountain top, then from far below on the river bank, and then

from the limb beside Gordo where the curassow really sat.

The little raccoon looked closely at the strange bird that could throw its voice so cleverly. He looked at the beautifully marked black and white feathers, at the strong feet and legs, and at the saucy curved topknot. At last he asked, "Why do you throw your voice here, there, and yonder, Mr. Ventriloquist?"

"To protect myself, my nest, and my family," replied the big curassow. "When a hungry raccoon or other animal starts toward my nest of eggs or young birds, I throw my 'oompas' on and on until he is led far away. But all the time I am right at home, ready to fight any snooping hawk or lizard that is watching my nest."

"How nice it must be to be a ventriloquist!" said Gordo. "I wish I had a ventriloquist to lead me out of this jungle growth, past the wild pineapple thickets and the jaguars, and onto the road that leads to the pyramids!"

"I'll do it," said the curassow.

"And I'll help you," said Papán.

Papán flew ahead and screamed when he saw a stealthy puma or a stalking jaguar. Then the clever curassow led the big beasts far astray with his well-placed "oompas." Gordo followed along with nothing to fear.

Finally they came to the road that led to the pyramids. There they said good-by to Gordo. With many a thank-you Gordo was off as fast as any fat little raccoon could go, and the hiccup bird and the ventriloquist of the woods returned to their mountain home.

CHAPTER 8 · The Rabbit in the Moon

It was almost dawn when Gordo met a shy little rabbit in his path.

"I don't see any trees around here, Little Rabbit. Do you know a good place for a raccoon to sleep?" asked Gordo.

Little Rabbit wiggled his nose and said, "Come with me, Gordo. I know where you can sleep!"

As they ran along, Gordo asked, "Do you know where any golden treasure is hidden, Little Rabbit?"

91

Little Rabbit blinked his eyes and said, "Golden treasure! I hear that there is much hidden treasure in Mexico, but I do not know where it is. The only gold I know about is in the sunflowers that march across the plains!"

"Very well. Come on," replied Gordo. "It is time for me to find a good bed. The man in the moon is putting the old moon to bed in the west, right now!"

"Oh, there is no man in the moon!" exclaimed Little Rabbit. "There is a rabbit in the moon!"

"How do you know there is a rabbit in the moon? Have you ever been to the moon?" asked Gordo.

"I have never been to the moon," said Little Rabbit, "but I have often seen the rabbit there when I have been playing in the moonlight. And I have heard the legend many times, too."

"Tell me this legend," said Gordo.

As the two made their way across a field of stiff, gray-green maguey plants, Little Rabbit told Gordo this legend of the rabbit in the moon:

"Long, long ago the sun was the only source of

light for the earth. Then in a struggle with the god of darkness, the sun-god was chipped and broken. The little pieces flew into space and became the moon and the stars.

"At first, the sun-god was pleased about the new bits of light that could shine on the earth when he was asleep for the night.

"After a time, the moon began to grow. Instead of the small narrow strip that it was in the beginning, it became a bright round disk in the sky.

"The sun-god then became jealous of the light of the moon. One night the great, round moon rose above the treetops before the sun-god had gone to bed. The angry sun-god looked around to find something to throw at the shining moon. The first thing he saw was a rabbit. He seized the rabbit and hurled it against the face of the moon to dim the moon's bright light.

"Until this very night, if you look closely, you can see the shadowy form of a rabbit, sprawled on the full moon's face."

93

"Oh, I like that legend," said Gordo, "but look, Little Rabbit—the moon is gone! That rabbit in the moon has pulled the moon into its burrow to sleep all through the day!"

"Yes," laughed Little Rabbit, "and right here among these maguey plants is a good place for you to sleep all through the day!"

As Gordo crept under the wide, spiny leaves of a large maguey plant, Little Rabbit cried, "Oh, no, not that one! The heart has been cut out of that plant, and a man will soon come to get the sweet juice that has collected in the hollow of the stalk. If the man should find you asleep here, he would take you home and eat you!"

"Oh, dear me!" exclaimed Gordo. "I did not know that people get sweet juice from the maguey plants!"

"Yes, they call the sweet juice honey water, and they make a very strong drink with it," replied Little Rabbit.

Gordo crept under a smaller maguey plant whose center stalk had not been cut. Just at daylight, before he had gone to sleep, he heard the echo of hoofs against the sun-baked ground.

Soon a man and a boy came, leading a burro. A big bag hung at each side of the burro. Each bag was made of the skin of a pig! The legs of the skins had been tied, leaving the only opening in the pigskin at the neck. The man carried a long, slender gourd with a hole at each end.

Gordo looked on in wonder as the man put one end of the gourd in his mouth and the other in the juice in the hollow of the maguey plant. When the man had sucked up a gourdful of the juice, he poured it into the limp pigskin bag. The skins grew fatter with each gourdful of juice. When the skins were quite full, the man, the boy, and the burro went on their way.

After they had gone with their pigskins full of honey water, Gordo settled down for the day's sleep. But before he went to sleep, he thought, "How glad I am that they don't use raccoon skins for their water bags!"

95

CHAPTER 9 · A New Face on an Old Temple

Many nights of roaming and many days of sleeping in strange places passed for Gordo. Then one dark, cool night he arrived at the Pyramid of the Sun.

Gordo gazed at the triangular-shaped pyramid rising two hundred feet or more in the air—the Pyramid of the Sun! About a half mile down the road he could see the smaller Pyramid of the Moon.

"I wonder where the golden treasure is hidden!" he said as he gazed at the steep, narrow steps leading up, up, up the side of the Pyramid of the Sun.

"Golden treasure? There is no golden treasure hidden here," said a voice near Gordo.

"Oh! You are Coati, the long-nosed coon, aren't you?" cried Gordo.

"Yes," replied Coati, "and here come my brothers and sisters."

Gordo was soon surrounded by the coatis. They were distant cousins of Gordo, and they were almost too friendly to suit him. They licked his face; they pulled his tail; they nipped his ears; and they asked more questions than a dozen Gordos could have answered.

The coatis' gray and tan bodies were longer than Gordo's body. Their tails were longer, too, and not as bushy as Gordo's. And they had long, pointed, upturned noses that gave them a queer, mischievous look.

The coatis are plentiful in Mexico. Gordo was glad to see them. They were playful and happy,

and they made good company for a lonesome raccoon. Gordo, however, had not intended to let
the coatis know that he was looking for a treasure,
for they liked all the good things to eat that he
liked. He was afraid he would get little of the
treasure if the coatis were along when he found it.

The leader of the coatis seemed to read Gordo's
mind. He said again, "There is no golden treasure
here, Gordo. You might find a treasure in Mexico
City, but not here. I play around these pyramids
every night, and I know what I'm talking about."

"Where do the steep steps lead?" asked Gordo.

"Only to the top of the pyramid where the Temple of the Sun once stood. But the temple and the huge statue of the sun-god were destroyed long, long years ago," replied Coati.

"I think I'll climb to the top," said Gordo. He started climbing the narrow steps, and several of the coatis went along, too. After climbing thirty-eight steep steps, Gordo reached a landing. Since he was tired, he sat on the landing for a time to rest.

"Come on, come on," called a coati from far above. "There are four more landings. You have many more steps to climb!"

The fat raccoon was almost out of breath when he finally reached the top. He sat and looked all around. He could see the Pyramid of the Moon and another smaller building which the coatis said was the Temple of Quetzalcoatl.

Seeing no place on the Pyramid of the Sun that looked as if it held hidden treasure, Gordo came down and went across to the Pyramid of the Moon.

On the ground around that pyramid he found some small bright pieces of pottery, a queer little stone figure of a man with a funny face, and a tiny stone figure of a jaguar's head.

"These can't be treasures, can they?" Gordo asked Coati.

"Oh, no, they are the little relics that the Indians scatter in their cornfields to bring good luck at harvest time," said Coati.

Gordo was weary and disappointed, but he went along with Coati to the small, square Temple of Quetzalcoatl. When they came near, Gordo saw the great carved stone figures that decorate the walls of the temple. He was so startled that he dropped the little relics he had brought from the Pyramid of the Moon.

"Those terrible dragons on the walls!" he exclaimed. "What are they?"

"Those are the figures of the feathered serpent," replied Coati. "They are serpents' heads with collars of feathers around them, all hand-carved from stone."

101

"Why are the ugly heads on the walls of the temple?" asked Gordo.

Coati replied, "This is the Temple of Quetzalcoatl. According to an old Indian legend, Quetzalcoatl was a great god who came from across the ocean to teach the Aztecs many valuable lessons. The emblem of Quetzalcoatl was a feathered serpent. That is why you see these figures on his temple."

Gordo knew nothing of the legendary Quetzalcoatl, and he was still a little afraid as he and Coati started to the underground rooms of the building.

Suddenly Coati cried, "Run, Gordo, run! Some-one is coming!"

Poor Gordo! He was fat, he was tired, and he didn't know which way to run! He heard voices and saw an Indian boy and an Indian man coming toward him.

The man stopped and picked up the small fig-ures of stone that Gordo had brought from the Pyramid of the Moon and had dropped on the ground near the Temple of Quetzalcoatl.

"Look, son," said the man to the boy, "this is the figure of the rain-god! We shall have good luck this year. Our corn will grow big and tall!"

The boy's attention was on something else. He cried, "Look, Father! What strange creature is that on the ground by the temple wall?"

"Well, let's see! Perhaps we can catch him," said the boy's father, as they started toward Gordo. Coati had disappeared, and Gordo was now all alone. He had to think fast or be caught. He

looked up at the strange feathered serpents and
decided to join them on the temple wall. He darted
into the shadows and then made his way quickly
and quietly up the wall to the nearest great, grin-
ning stone face.

Gordo flattened his body on top of the ugly stone
head. He could almost imagine that the dragon
turned its eyes to watch him and gritted its huge
white teeth. But what Gordo heard was only the

beating of his own little heart, and certainly the old stone eyes did not move!

After looking all around the temple and poking into all the hiding places on the ground, the Indians decided that the little animal had run away. As they walked away, the boy looked back at the old Temple of Quetzalcoatl.

"Look, Father!" he cried. "There is a new face on the old temple! I never did see that one before! That serpent's head does not look like the others! See, it seems to be wearing a funny fur cap!"

"It does look a little strange," said the father. "We shall come back tomorrow and take a good look at it in the daylight."

Gordo sighed with relief as the Indians passed out of sight.

"There'll be no new face on the old temple when they come back!" he said to himself as he scrambled down from the old stone head. "There is no golden treasure here, and I am leaving this spooky old place right now!"

CHAPTER 10 · Tricks and Treats

When he left the Pyramid of the Sun and the Pyramid of the Moon, Gordo was feeling discouraged about finding the hidden treasure. Too, in his dreams he could see the terrible feathered serpents of the Temple of Quetzalcoatl. He knew now that he should never have left home. But since he had come so far, he kept wandering on and on.

107

"Everyone seems to believe there is hidden treasure, but no one seems to know where to look for it. It is not as easy to find as I thought it would be," Gordo muttered. He thought of all the places in which he had been told to look for the golden treasure. "It's in the village; it's in the desert; it's in the pyramids; it's in the wild pineapple thicket. Now, Coati says it's in Mexico City!"

Gordo usually traveled through the woods and over the plains instead of along the highways and through the villages. He visited with coatis, squirrels, monkeys, and other raccoons along the way. Sometimes he would get a ride on an Indian's oxcart. One morning he climbed into one of the big pots that a man was carrying in a frame on his back. It was nearly daylight when Gordo stowed away in the pot. He was tired and soon fell asleep.

When Gordo waked, the man was unloading the pots at a village market. The afternoon siesta was over in the village, and people were hurrying about the streets. Although the sun was still shining,

Gordo knew that he must get out of the pot and find a safer hiding place.

While the man was carrying some of the pots to a market stall on the sidewalk, Gordo climbed out of his hiding place and hurried away to a big tree that stood in the village plaza. From his perch high in the tree he could look down on the busy little streets.

Since Gordo had no calendar, he could not know that it was Halloween, or The Feast of the Dead as it is called in Mexico.

The market place was full of little shops and sidewalk stalls, all filled with things to sell—clothes, foods, pots, and toys. People were coming and going, buying and selling, visiting and laughing. Gordo thought he had never seen such a busy place.

A big gray squirrel joined Gordo in his tree. The squirrel looked at Gordo and asked, "What are you doing here, Mr. Raccoon?"

"I am seeking a hidden treasure," replied Gordo.

"There is no hidden treasure here," said the

squirrel. "You might find some old Mayan treasure in the far south, but not here. My cousin Negrito, the black squirrel, told me that he had seen the places where rich treasures of gold and jade are hidden. You will have to travel far, far from here to find them."

"Travel, travel! Far, far!" muttered Gordo.

The fat raccoon looked down again upon the busy streets of the village. He turned to the squirrel and asked, "Why are the people rushing about down there?"

"Oh, they are getting ready for The Feast of the Dead!" said the squirrel. "Tomorrow is All Saints' Day."

"Yes—and if they catch me, I'll probably be both the feast and the dead!" thought Gordo.

The more Gordo thought about the feast, the hungrier he became. Late in the afternoon the church bells began to ring. Since there were not so many people on the streets then, Gordo decided to go down and see what he could find to eat.

He kept out of sight in the shadows for some

time, but at last his curiosity led him into a little shop. There was no one around. He might have had a good time if his curiosity had not been too great.

A strange object lying on a chair especially interested him. This object had little black buttons at one end. It had a hole in the middle with strings drawn across it.

"This is a funny thing," thought Gordo.

He took hold of the little black buttons and twisted them. They would not come off. He nibbled at them but could not bite into them.

"Perhaps if I pull a string, it will open a door and I shall find food inside," he thought. He took one of the strings in his nimble fingers and pulled.

"Twang!" went the string of the guitar, and two boys came running.

"Look, look!" called one boy. "It is Gordo, the fat fellow, and he is playing a Halloween trick on us!"

The boys thought it great fun that Gordo had played the guitar. They ran to get food for him, but poor Gordo was so frightened by the sound of the guitar and the laughter of the boys that he ran outside and missed their treat.

While racing away from the boys, Gordo came to a high iron fence with a big iron gate. Through the gate he could see pretty flowers and a bubbling fountain in the patio.

"I could find butterflies over those flowers," he said to himself. "And oh, how I would like to play in that water! There is a latch on this gate, but I know I can open it."

With such a clever mind and such nimble fingers, Gordo could make his way into a place almost as easily as a person could. He climbed up the iron gate and lifted the latch. As the heavy gate swung open, he jumped down inside the patio.

First of all he went to the fountain. To his great surprise and delight, he saw dozens of goldfish in the pool of the fountain.

"Oh, what a treat!" he cried as he slapped the

little fish out of the pool and ate them. "These are not hidden treasures, perhaps, but they are golden treasures worth while!" he said as he licked his lips.

Gordo should have been satisfied with his goldfish supper, but he saw a half-open door and decided to look inside the house. Then came his downfall!

A black dog saw Gordo and rushed out barking. A boy and a girl followed, and the chase was on.

Poor Gordo tried to hide. He crouched among the red geraniums, but the black dog sniffed him out. He climbed a vine-covered trellis, but the boy shook him down. He crept inside a box by the steps. The girl covered the box with a board, and for the first time in his life Gordo was trapped.

Some time later, the children placed a brick on the board covering Gordo's box. Then they went to the market place, taking the dog with them.

Gordo jumped and clawed at the board until finally he pushed it off and escaped from the box. He ran along the porch in the shadows toward the big iron gate.

Just as he was ready to jump from the porch, Gordo found a strange little black box. He knew that he should hurry on, but his curiosity persuaded him to stop and examine the box. A small blue ball was fastened in a round, shiny pan at one end of the box. Gordo turned the black box over and over, but he could not open it.

"Oh, here is the latch," he said gleefully, as he noticed a small, tongue-like pin on the front of the box. "This should open the box!"

Gordo pressed the pin, and—poof!—a very bright light flashed over and all around him.

The light almost blinded the little raccoon for a moment. Then he rushed to the fence and scrambled over, not even waiting to open the big iron gate. Not once did he look back to see if the big flash had set fire to the place. And never would he know what surprise and fun the children would have when they found among their next set of pictures the likeness of a funny, fat raccoon wearing a black mask.

"Too many tricks!" exclaimed Gordo, as he hur-

116

ried along the street. "I'll return to the woods. Tomorrow I must go on to Mexico City."

Just then Gordo came to a toy shop. He stopped and gazed in wonder at the queer little toy skeletons made of gold wire. Then he shook his head and mumbled, "The Feast of the Dead—ugh!"

In the next stall Gordo saw something that interested him more than the skeletons. That little shop was a sweetshop. In it were many little figures made of white sugar and decorated with pink and blue and gold. There were sugar burros with gold strings around their necks. There was a sugar pig with a curly pink tail. A sugar goat with gold horns wore a blue paper frill.

Gordo tasted a sugar cat with gold eyes and then settled down for a big meal of the sugar goodies. When he could eat no more, he waddled off to the woods, thinking, "What a treat! And they call it The Feast of the Dead!"

CHAPTER 11 • Bedtime Stories

Night after night Gordo traveled toward Mexico City. He asked all the animals he met where to look for the hidden treasure. Each one told him of a different place, and poor Gordo became more and more puzzled.

One night Gordo ate supper with a slim little monkey named Flaco. Beside the fat raccoon, Flaco looked smaller than usual. He seemed to be all legs and arms.

119

Gordo liked Flaco because the slender little monkey knew where to find ripe fruit. He also led Gordo to some good nuts and helped him dig some turtle eggs out of the mud.

After a midnight supper one night, Gordo heard a mockingbird singing in the top of the big old cypress tree in which he and Flaco were spending the night.

"Why does the mockingbird sing at night? Other birds don't sing much after dark," said Gordo.

"The mockingbird has so many voices that it can't use them all in the day," replied Flaco. "It is called the bird with four hundred voices. I know a legend about it."

"Tell me the legend," said Gordo. "I want to know more about the bird with four hundred voices."

The little monkey then told Gordo this legend:

"Long, long ago, a trader was returning from a distant trip to his home in Mexico City.

"As he passed through the jungle, he heard the most beautiful singing in the world. He went to see who could be singing so sweetly and found that the music came from the throat of a shy maiden with skin as fair as the gardenia blossoms.

"The trader fell in love with the beautiful maiden, who could sing four hundred different songs. When they were married, he took her to his home in the city. There he gave her jewels, fine clothes, and all kinds of riches. But the lovely maiden, like the rarest birds and the fairest orchids, longed for her woodland home.

"When the trader was returning from his next trip, he again heard the beautiful singing in the jungle. He looked and found not a maiden but a slender gray and white bird.

"When the trader reached home, he was told that the maiden had died from grief and that her soul had flown out the window in the form of a graceful gray and white bird.

"The trader was very sad, but soon he heard the sweet singing again. When he looked, he saw the mockingbird flirting its gray and white wings and rising into the air for joy as it sang.

"Then the man knew that all through the day, and even in the still of night, he could always hear the sweet voice of his loved one in the songs of the mockingbird—the bird with four hundred voices."

"I like that story," said Gordo. "I like the four hundred songs of the mockingbird, and I like this great old cypress tree, too. It must have lived a long time to grow so very large."

"Oh, yes, probably hundreds of years!" said the little monkey. "The natives call the cypress trees 'ahuehuetes.' They have a legend about the ahuehuete trees, too."

122

"I should also like to hear that legend," replied Gordo.

Flaco scratched his neck, chewed at his fingernail, and began his story:

"In the very earliest days in Mexico, the people wandered far in search of a happy land where there would be fresh water, shade trees, and plenty of food.

"They became so tired and weary that they camped for a while on a bare, rocky plain where there were no shade trees. The only foods they could find were cactus fruits, small sprouts of chili peppers, and a few lizards and grasshoppers.

"One day the daughter of the leader of the tribe asked the sun-god to give her people a place where they could settle down. They were weary from their long wandering and their searching for food.

"The sun-god told her that her people might settle down where they were. In a few days the rains came, and food became more plentiful. But still there were no trees to shade the people from the hot summer sun.

"One bright morning a messenger came from Quetzalcoatl, the Aztec god of the day and the air. The messenger told the leader's daughter that he had brought someone to speak to her. When the maiden turned around, she saw an old man with snow-white hair.

" 'I am Señor Ahuehuetzin,' said the old man. 'I have brought you a gift—my hair. The sun-god says that you should plant it, a hair here and a hair there. Soon the hairs will grow and give shade to your people.'

"The young girl was puzzled, but she did as the old man said. She took the hairs and planted them here and there around the village. In a short time they grew and became huge cypress trees like this one in which we are sitting.

"The people were so happy with the deep shade of the big trees that they called them 'ahuehuetes' in memory of the kind old man."

It was nearly daylight when Flaco finished the legend. Gordo liked his stories and asked for more.

"It is time for my breakfast and time for you to

go to bed," said the little monkey. "I'll tell you another story when we meet again."

"Before you leave, won't you tell me where you think I might find a hidden treasure?" begged Gordo.

The monkey thought and thought. At last he said, "There are many stories of hidden treasure, but I do not know where the treasure really is. There is a very old wishing well not far from Mexico City. Some say that great treasures were thrown into the well when the Spanish invaders came, but I do not know whether that is true or not."

"Thank you very much," said Gordo. "I shall go by the wishing well and see what I can find. Goodby, Flaco. You have been good company."

As Gordo curled up on the big limb of the old ahuehuete tree, the slender little monkey went swinging off to catch his breakfast of insects.

CHAPTER 12 · A Wish Comes True

The wishing well stood at the edge of a little village not far from Mexico City. It was a queer old well. The square walls were made of stone. Steep, narrow steps led down to the water. The clear, shallow water seemed to come from an underground spring. It bubbled merrily over the flat stone that formed the bottom of the well.

127

Gordo peeped into the well, but he could see very little in the dim morning light. Since no one was around at such at early hour, he decided to go down the steps to the bottom.

He waded in the shallow water and ran his sensitive little hands across the rock bottom. The small coins he found did not interest him.

"Just as I feared—no treasure!" said Gordo. "I'll drop these coins back into the well and wish I could find the treasure I seek."

Moving nearer the wall of the old well, Gordo ran his hand far back under the wall. "Here is something bigger than those coins!" he cried. "Here are two things!" He closed his hand over the objects and brought them out.

One object was a large gold coin with strange
markings on it. The other was a disk of gold about
the size of a dollar. It was in the shape of a jumping frog. Gordo washed the objects in the bubbling water and tried to eat them. They had no
taste and were so hard that his teeth could not
break them.

"I'd like a golden treasure I could eat," muttered the fat raccoon as he climbed out of the old wishing well. He shook the water from his coat and started on his way to Mexico City. As he ran along, still carrying the gold objects in his mouth, he thought about the strange wishes that people must make at the wishing well.

"I wonder what wish was made when this gold frog was thrown into the well," thought Gordo. "Was the wish for treasure or for love? Was it for happiness or health? Was it for food or freedom?"

Gordo rolled his tongue over the objects in his mouth and chuckled, "Perhaps it was a raccoon like me who dropped the gold frog into the well! If so, he probably wished that the thing would turn into a plump live frog that he could eat for supper!"

It was daylight when Gordo finally entered the big city. He had never been in a big city before, and already he was seeing many things that he would like to examine.

"I must throw away these pieces of gold and

130

find a safe place to sleep in the sun until the night comes down over the city," he said.

On the sidewalk he saw a blind beggar holding out his hand for whatever anyone might give him. Gordo stood on his hind legs and looked into the beggar's hand to see whether he was offering food. He saw that there was nothing at all in the beggar's thin hand.

"Perhaps he has a wish to make! A coin that is taken from the wishing well should have as much magic as one that is thrown into the well," thought Gordo.

The little raccoon wrinkled his funny black mask and took the coin and the golden frog from his mouth. He took one last look at them and then dropped them into the beggar's hand. As Gordo whirled to run away, his long bushy tail brushed the beggar's face.

The fat raccoon disappeared so quickly that he never knew what a commotion he caused. And he never knew that he made the blind man's wish come true.

While Gordo was racing out of the city to hide

away for his day's sleep, the blind man was calling his daughter, "María! María! Come here quickly! A miracle has happened! Here in the early dawn, the great Quetzalcoatl has visited me! He has left something in my hand, and his great feathered serpent brushed my face as he passed!"

"Oh, Father, this is very strange! I shall call our good neighbor, Señor Hidalgo!" cried María.

When Señor Hidalgo looked at the strange coin and the golden frog, he said, "It is like a miracle, my good friend! These objects are very valuable! This old Spanish coin is one of the most ancient yet found in Mexico! The golden frog is probably an old Mayan prayer offering! You will never have to beg any more, my friend. The National Museum will pay you a great sum of money for these objects!"

"I was never so excited before!" cried the blind man. "Now I can pay for an operation on my eyes! When I can see to work, María and I shall be happy again! Yes, my dearest wish has come true!"

CHAPTER 13 · Gordo and the Blue Pig

"Oh, how pretty! How wonderful!" Gordo cried. He had come to the floating gardens of Xochimilco, the place of the flowers. Almost everything a raccoon could want—water, trees, flowers, vegetables—could be found here. Already Gordo could hear the familiar splash of a frog in the canal. He could see the trails left in the mud by worms and snails. He could smell the fragrance of many flowers and, better still, the fragrance of red beans and chicken cooking and of tortillas toasting in the little thatched homes of the Indians.

135

"Good places to sleep and good things to eat! I shall stay here a long time," thought Gordo.

One morning very early Gordo saw an Indian woman paddling a small wooden canoe on the canal. When the little boat came near, he could see that it was piled high with flowers of many colors. There were pink sweet peas, purple violets, yellow and white daisies, red carnations, and many other flowers.

"I'll just take a ride on that boat before I go to sleep for the day," said Gordo to himself.

He jumped into the back of the canoe and hid under a big bunch of carnations. As the woman paddled the boat down the canal, Gordo saw strips of land where vegetables were growing and others that were planted with flowers. Back among the tall trees, he could see the small thatched houses where the people lived.

The people at Xochimilco grew most of the flowers and vegetables that were used in Mexico City, even as they do today. The Indian woman with her boatload of flowers had started to the market. When she turned her boat into the main canal, Gordo jumped into the canal with a splash; for he did not want to leave this place where food was so plentiful.

Xochimilco was all that Gordo had thought it would be. He had so much fun playing in the tall trees and hunting along the canal banks that he stayed a long time, almost forgetting that he was on a treasure hunt. One day when he was scratching insects out of a rotten log, a little opossum swung down by its tail from a limb and called to Gordo, "What are you looking for?"

"Right now I am looking for supper," said Gordo. "But what I'd really like to find is a hidden treasure. Where do you think I might find a hidden treasure in Mexico City?"

The opossum pulled himself back upon the limb and said, "It all depends upon the kind of treasure you seek. Treasures are funny things. To some people, coins are treasures; to some, jewels are treasures; to some, toys are treasures. To the farmer, a burro is a treasure; to the bullfighter, the ears of the bull he has killed are treasures; to a jaguar, a young fawn is a treasure; to me, birds' eggs are treasures. What kind of treasure do you seek?"

"Oh!" said Gordo. "The special treasure that I

am seeking is a hidden golden treasure. I think
it is something to eat—something very delicious!"

"Well, as this is the Christmas season, you will
probably find many delicious things in the city—
if you don't get caught while looking for them!"
replied the opossum. Then he let himself down
by the tail and disappeared in a bed of flowers.

Gordo decided to make a trip through the city. He rambled around for days, but he did not find any hidden treasure. One day he met a friendly gray squirrel in a tree. The squirrel led Gordo to a big park where many birds, frogs, and insects were to be found.

"You have been such a good friend that I think I shall call you Amigo," said Gordo.

"Good! I like to be called Amigo," replied the friendly squirrel. "Come with me and see the city!"

Amigo guided Gordo out of the big park. For awhile they sat together on a balcony where they could watch a great party—a fiesta.

"I like the bright dresses that the girls wear! And I like the trim suits and bright sashes that the boys wear, too!" cried Gordo.

"Yes, the fiesta costumes are very colorful," said Amigo. "But come, now. There is much more to see, and I want to take you to the market before you leave the city. We may find something good in the market!"

Amigo led Gordo on and on. At one spot, seeing

140

a dog on the street, they jumped through an open window into a big building and hid behind a huge, round stone.

"I wonder why this big stone is in here," whispered Gordo.

"This is the famous old Calendar Stone of the Aztecs," replied Amigo.

"Oh! Did the Aztecs use a stone for a calendar?" Gordo asked as he walked to the front of the stone and gazed at the strange figures carved on it.

"Yes," replied Amigo, "it was their way of calculating time. I have heard that some of these funny little faces and figures on the stone represented the twenty days of the Aztec month and the eighteen months of the Aztec year. But come along! They don't mean a thing to you and me. The food in the market means more to us!"

The two little animals hurried along the streets toward the market place. As they passed the famous ring where the bullfights are held, Gordo saw something bright beside the wall.

"Look, Amigo! I have found a fairy wand!" he exclaimed. "Now if I can find the fairy, perhaps she can tell me where the golden treasure is hidden!"

Gordo held the long, slender wand in his hand and turned it over and over. The slender stick was gaily frilled with pink paper, but it had a very sharp point that was winged like a fishhook.

142

"Oh, dear, no!" exclaimed Amigo. "That is no fairy wand! That is a banderilla!"

"A banderilla? What is a banderilla?" asked Gordo.

"If you ever had one stuck into your neck, you would know!" replied the squirrel. "A banderilla is a little dart decorated with paper frills. It is stuck into the neck of the bull at a bullfight to make the bull angry. No animal wants a banderilla stuck into its neck!"

"I certainly don't want a banderilla in my neck!" said the fat raccoon as he dropped the gaily decorated dart on the ground.

Soon Gordo and his friend reached the market place. Every shop was gay with holiday decorations. There were straw cowboys; there were dolls in bright fiesta costumes; there were big, colorful hats; and there were many bright baskets and blankets.

The objects that attracted Gordo's attention were some queer, big paper figures in many shapes

and colors. The paper figures were hanging by strings on the wall, high over the sidewalk.

"That's funny!" said Amigo. "These piñatas are already filled and ready to deliver to someone's home!"

Gordo looked again at the big paper figures. One was a green and white burro. One was a big red tomato. One was a fluffy pink carnation. Then, at the very end of the wall, Gordo found the funniest one of all—a fat blue paper pig!

144

"What are the piñatas good for? What are they filled with?" asked Gordo.

"They're good for a big surprise and lots of fun at Christmas," replied Amigo. "They are filled with toys and with all kinds of goodies! Breaking the piñata is a great game for the children. There is a thin clay jar inside the paper figure. The toys and goodies are in the jar. Each child is blindfolded and given a stick with which he tries to break the piñata. The piñata swings back and forth on its string and is hard to hit by the blindfolded child. Finally, some child breaks the jar, and the goodies fall all over the place!"

"Oh, my! That is a good game! I wish we could break a piñata and get all the goodies!" said Gordo.

"That would be fun," agreed Amigo.

"I know what we can do," said Gordo. "We can jump upon a piñata. We are so big that the string will break. The piñata will crash on the sidewalk, and we can get the goodies!"

"This will be fun!" cried Amigo. "Which piñata shall we break?"

"The blue pig!" said Gordo. "It is the funniest one, and it is the fattest one, too!"

The two little animals laughed as they leaped upon the blue pig piñata. Crash! It hit the sidewalk with Gordo and Amigo piled up on top! Out rolled the goodies—candies, nuts, sugar cane, tops, whistles, and many other things!

146

Before they could pick themselves up, the shop-keeper came running. He scolded Gordo and struck at the squirrel. The little fellows had to run for their lives and did not get to eat any of the goodies that were scattered around them.

"Good-by, Gordo. I must go home now," said the squirrel, racing away.

"Good-by, Amigo, and thanks for being such a good friend. It was fun to break the piñata, even if we didn't get the goodies!" said Gordo.

The squirrel raced out of sight down the street. Gordo slipped back and hid under a big red and yellow hat until the shopkeeper took all the piñatas inside the shop and closed the door.

As Gordo crept out from under the hat, he grabbed a handful of beans from a jar on the side-walk.

"I couldn't get the blue pig's goodies, but I'll at least have beans for supper," he said as he made his way out of the city.

CHAPTER 14 • Christmas in the Air

"No hidden treasure," sighed Gordo. "I seemed to find everything in the city but the treasure. Now I shall go far to the south and search until the hidden treasure is mine!"

Gordo was on his way out of the city with its noisy streets, its bright tiled roofs, and its gay people when he passed a place where glass was blown. In the window he saw many interesting pieces of glass. There were blue glass dishes, and there were all kinds of blown glass figures. Gordo liked the little figures of animals, birds, and flowers— some of them not any bigger than the beans he had taken from the shopkeeper's jar.

Farther on he came to a place where all sizes and kinds of pots were shaped and baked. He peeped into a house where colorful blankets were woven. Finally, he crawled into a big red, green, and yellow basket that he found sitting on the sidewalk. There he fell asleep among the oranges and potatoes that it held.

150

Gordo waked up with a bumpity-bump! The man who had been jogging along with the basket on his back had set it down on the ground with a bump.

"This basket is heavier than it was before I sold the eggs I had in it!" exclaimed the man as he looked into the basket.

Gordo knew that it was time for him to move on! He leaped out of the basket and scampered up a tree while the man shouted and scolded.

After dark, Gordo came down from the tree and started on his way. As he ran along in the moonlight, he saw someone coming toward him. Gordo raised the fur on his back and growled, "Stay where you are!"

The big, rusty red wildcat hissed. Then, seeing that it was only Gordo in her path, she called, "Oh, hello, Gordo! You are not going to fight me, are you? I am Eyra, the wildcat. We should be friends."

"Oh, Eyra, I did not know that it was you. I know some of your relatives. I hunted field mice

151

and little birds in the same underbrush with one of your brothers. Why don't you come along with me?"

Eyra was a long-tailed wildcat. Her short legs and creeping walk gave her a slinky look. Some animals hunt in the day, and some, like Gordo, hunt at night. But Eyra would hunt either in the daylight or in the dark.

She looked at Gordo a minute before replying, "Where are you going? What are you hunting?"

152

"I am going far to the south to search for a hidden treasure," said Gordo.

"Hidden treasure? Where do you think you'll find it?" asked Eyra.

"I wish I knew!" said Gordo. "I'd like to find it and go back home. I didn't expect to have to come so far to find it."

"I think we should look for supper first," said Eyra.

"I have some beans, but they are very hard,"
said Gordo, and he put on the ground the beans
that he had taken after the piñata crashed. "I have
carried them in my mouth ever since I left the city,
but they are still very hard. Perhaps if we wash
them, they will become soft enough to eat."

154

As he spoke—pip! One of the beans popped into the air. Then, pip, pip! Away jumped two more of the beans. Gordo started to put his hand over the others, but—pip!—one almost popped into his face!

Gordo was surprised and startled, but Eyra laughed and laughed. "Those are Mexican jumping beans, Gordo," she said. "They are not good to eat. Come on! I know where we can find a good supper. The moon is rising high over Popo and Ixta, and we should be on our way."

"See how white the tops of the volcanoes are," said Gordo. "It looks as if Popo is smoking! See!"

"Yes," said Eyra, "the volcanoes are capped with snow. The mists over Popo look like smoke. Popo's real name is Popocatépetl, and that means 'The Smoking Mountain.' Ixta's real name is Ixtacíhuatl. Ixtacíhuatl means 'The Sleeping Woman.' An old Aztec legend says that Popo watches over Ixta while she sleeps. When the snow is deep and the air becomes very cold, he blows his hot breath across her, to keep her warm."

155

"Look!" said Gordo. "I see Popo's hot breath rising in the air! Ixta will not be cold tonight!"

Eyra led Gordo to a little village. "It is the

156

Christmas season," she told him. "We should find
good things to eat here in the village."

Gordo remembered the trouble with the piñatas
and was a little afraid to go into any town again.

"Come on," said Eyra. "I see a Mexican flag, and
that is a good sign that we shall find a delicious
supper."

Gordo looked at the flag with its three bars of
red, white, and green. When he was closer to the
flag, he saw on it the picture of an eagle holding
a snake in its mouth.

"Why does the flag have a picture of an eagle and a snake on it?" he asked Eyra.

"Oh, that is the good sign," said Eyra. "Don't you see that the eagle is having a delicious supper?"

"It may be a good sign for the eagle, but what about the poor snake!" said Gordo.

"I will tell you the legend," said Eyra; and this is the legend she told him:

"In early times the friendly gods of the Aztecs promised the people that they should have a richer and more beautiful land than that in which they were then living. They were told that they should travel until they found an eagle sitting on a cactus plant and holding a serpent in its beak.

"After traveling far to the south, they found a big lake. In the lake was an island. On the island the people saw an eagle on a cactus plant holding a serpent in its beak.

"They knew that they had found the right place. They ended their travels and built a great city on
158

the island in the lake. That great city is now the capital of Mexico."

"Oh, I see!" said Gordo. "The eagle with a snake was a good sign for the Aztecs. I wish I had a good sign to lead me to the hidden treasure I seek!"

"I see a good sign for supper," said Eyra, as she crept toward a coop with a rooster in it.

"I can open the door!" cried Gordo.

"Good! This rooster will make a fine supper for both of us," said Eyra.

Gordo opened the door and reached his hand inside to catch the rooster. But he did not catch the rooster! Instead he cried, "Ouch, ouch! He has stuck a banderilla in me!"

The rooster was ready for a cockfight, with his sharp metal spur in place. When Gordo reached inside the coop, the old fighting cock spurred the surprised raccoon on the shoulder.

Eyra did not know what had happened, but she did know that Gordo's cry would bring the owner of the cock running. Calling good-by to Gordo, she went slinking around the house and disappeared in a big avocado tree.

Gordo also hurried out of sight and found a good hiding place on the roof of a shed. When he started down later, he noticed a big stack of box-like frames by the side of the shed. The frames were made of sections of bamboo and were in many different shapes and sizes.

"I wonder what these things are!" he thought as he examined first one and then another.

As he turned to leave, he saw some other pieces of bamboo burning on a pile of trash near by. He thought, "They forgot to burn these. I'll do it for them." He brought a blazing section of bamboo from the fire and held it to one of the frames.

"Z-z-z! F-f-sh! Bang! Boom!"

The place was suddenly aglow with yellow, blue, red, and green fireworks. Into the air flew all kinds of fiery figures—pinwheels, stars, a bull's head, and even a Mexican flag!

"Now what have I done!" cried Gordo in amazement.

160

The little raccoon did not know that the bamboo frames were for the village fireworks. He did not know that the hollow bamboo sections were filled with gunpowder. He knew only that everyone in the village had rushed out to see what had happened.

The people looked at the bright figures flashing in the night sky and cried, "Our Christmas fireworks! They have all been set off! Our Christmas is all in the air!"

Gordo did not look back to see what happened, for he knew that his Christmas celebrating was finished. When he finally got out of the village, he was out of breath and quite ready to go to bed without any supper.

CHAPTER 15 · The First Cornfield

For weeks after the fireworks trick Gordo stayed
away from the towns. He visited with coatis and
made friends of the monkeys and squirrels along
the way. Day after day he was drawing nearer
and nearer to the tropical jungles in the southern
part of Mexico.

Early one morning Gordo climbed into a giant
ahuehuete tree to spend the day sleeping. A black
squirrel raced across the limbs of the big old tree,
and called, "Welcome to my ahuehuete tree!"

163

"Hello!" replied Gordo. Then he added, "My, you are really a black squirrel!"

Gordo recalled the story that Rojo had told him of the three brown squirrels who had brought the first fire treasure to the earth. He had hardly believed that there were really black squirrels, as Rojo had said. Now he knew it was true, for here was a black squirrel right by his side, chattering and asking him questions.

"I am Negrito," said the black squirrel. "I live here in this tree. Where did you come from? I don't see many raccoons like you around here. I see coatis and honey bears, and sometimes a ring-tailed cat. But I don't often see a raccoon with a mask like yours."

"I came from farther north," said Gordo, "and I am going to travel still farther to the south. I am seeking a hidden treasure. Someone told me that you know where rich treasures are hidden."

"Oh, yes, there are all kinds of treasures hidden near here. Not far away there are strange old mounds in which people find many treasures of

164

the past. I have seen them take many objects out
of the mounds—gold necklaces, gold figures of lizards and turtles, small jaguars made of jade, silver
and crystal vases—all kinds of treasures."

"That is where I want to go. How do I get
there?" asked Gordo.

"Here comes Manito. He goes there often, and
I am sure he will show you the way," said Negrito.
The little black squirrel arched his fluffy black tail,
waved at the little creature who was coming down
from the treetop, and then bounded off to disappear among the leaves of the old cypress tree.

Gordo looked up and saw a lively little animal
scampering about in the treetop. Soon it was sitting beside Gordo and gazing at him with big,
black eyes.

"My, my, Manito!" exclaimed Gordo. "Are you a squirrel or a monkey?"

"I am a squirrel monkey," laughed Manito.

This squirrel monkey was a cunning little animal about ten inches long. He had a long, furry tail that was several inches longer than his body, but unlike other Mexican monkeys the squirrel monkey cannot hold things with his tail. Manito's fur was brownish gray on his body and almost golden on his arms. The skin of his face was pale except for a circular patch around his nose and mouth. This circular patch was deep blue-black. His pale ears drooped at the top and were tufted with gray hair.

Manito smiled and said, "Welcome to my ahuehuete tree!"

"Your ahuehuete tree? Negrito said it was his ahuehuete tree!" exclaimed Gordo.

"Negrito's, Manito's—it doesn't matter. This old tree is big enough for all of us to claim it," replied the squirrel monkey.

166

"I guess you are right," said Gordo. "It is the biggest tree that I have ever seen."

"Yes, this old ahuehuete tree is probably the biggest tree in the world. People say it is many hundreds of years old. I have heard that twenty-eight people touching fingers can barely reach around its trunk!" said Manito.

"Yes, it is such a wonderful old tree that I think I shall claim it, too," said Gordo, "at least for today!"

"Where are you going after today?" Manito asked.

"I want to go to the ancient mounds and look for hidden treasure," Gordo replied. "Will you please show me the way?"

"Oh, you will not be safe there, Gordo!" exclaimed Manito. "Men are digging, digging, digging there all the time. They guard the place day and night. You would probably find yourself in their dinner pot if you went there!"

"But the treasure—" began Gordo.

"Go farther on. Go on to the coast," replied

Manito. "The flamingos say the greatest treasures of all are buried deep in the jungles there. Perhaps the flamingos will guide you to the place."

"Thank you for telling me, Manito. I shall start to the coast tonight," said Gordo.

While the two animals were talking, Gordo saw a man working in a cleared spot on a hillside. The man was making holes in the ground with a sharp-pointed stick.

168

"Look, Manito! Do you think that man is digging for hidden treasure?" asked Gordo.

Manito laughed and showed two rows of little teeth which looked very white between his red tongue and his blue-black lips. "No, Gordo," he said, "that man is planting corn. If you watch closely, you can see him drop a seed or two into each hole."

169

"Is that the way they plant their corn?" asked Gordo. "In Xochimilco I saw tiny green shoots, like wide blades of grass, which the Indians called corn. In a village I saw women grinding the yellow grains between two rocks, and the grains looked hard and tasteless. This is the first time I ever saw corn planted. I suppose someday the seed will grow and make a cornfield on that hillside."

"Did you ever hear how the very first cornfield was started in Mexico?" asked the little squirrel monkey.

"No, but I should like to hear about it," replied Gordo.

Manito settled himself on the limb of the tree and wrapped his long tail around his neck. Then he told Gordo the Aztec legend of the first cornfield:

"Long, long ago, Quetzalcoatl, the great Aztec god of the day, came to visit with the Indians. He saw how poor they were and what plain homes they had. He wanted to do something to help them.

170

"Quetzalcoatl was very wise. He knew how to mine and cut precious stones. He knew how to gather and string coral. He knew how to work silver and gold. He knew how to make pretty pottery and tiles. He could weave fine cloth and could even make beautiful tapestry with feathers.

"Soon Quetzalcoatl built beautiful houses of silver and gold for his people. He decorated them with jewels and fine tapestries. But even after he had given the people all these riches, Quetzalcoatl still was not satisfied with the condition of his people. He wanted to give them something more useful and more lasting than gold and jewels. He wanted to give them something good to eat—something that they could have fresh, year after year, long after he had gone away.

"One night he climbed to the top of a hill and sat down in the moonlight to think about his people's needs. He was tired and soon fell asleep. In a dream he saw a strange anthill with workers running here and there. Soon a worker arrived with a large yellow grain.

171

"Then in his dream Quetzalcoatl saw a strange land where the fields were covered with tall plants. Among the long, waving green leaves of the plants were big ears of grain with golden, silky tassels hanging from them like the sun-god's golden hair.

"Quetzalcoatl went at once to find the anthill that he had seen in his dream. When he found it, he changed himself into a big red ant and entered the anthill. There he found the big yellow grains and carried several of them away to his people.

"He gave the grains to the people and told them to plant them. The people made holes in the ground with pointed sticks and planted the grains. The seeds grew, and soon the field was full of waving green corn. That was the country's first cornfield!

"When Quetzalcoatl saw how pleased the people were with their corn, he knew that he had given them the best gift in the world; and he went away happy."

"Oh, my! And they are still planting corn!" exclaimed Gordo.

172

"Yes," said Manito, "for hundreds of years the natives of Mexico have continued to plant the seeds of corn in the hillsides with pointed sticks. When the green shoot grows and the tasseled ears develop, they gather the harvest in baskets. Later the grains are ground into corn meal on small grinding stones. The women then make the corn meal into dough and the dough into good tortillas for their families to eat."

Gordo was delighted with Manito's story of the first cornfield and of how the natives harvested their corn. He looked at the funny little squirrel monkey and said, "Someday I am going to examine those yellow grains of corn, even though they do look as hard as jumping beans!"

Then Gordo and Manito curled up for a nap in the old ahuehuete tree, as others had done for hundreds of years before.

CHAPTER 16 · Flamingo's Red Coat

When Gordo left the old cypress tree, he hurried away to find the flamingos. He traveled far and even dared to travel some in the daylight. One day he was completely lost in the jungle growth. He sat at noon in a tropical tree and looked at the bright colors of the jungle.

Orchids of many colors bloomed in the trees. Strange birds in bright-colored coats were taking their rest in the deep jungle forest. Brilliant green and yellow flies drifted lazily in the air. A big swarm of deep-blue butterflies hovered over the blossoms of a tropical tree. A group of yellow-headed parrots nodded and mumbled over the day's gossip. Two quiet anteaters in brown and tan coats licked up ants at the foot of a tree. Except for the cracking of nuts by two black squirrels, there was a deep silence over the jungle. It was so quiet that Gordo soon fell asleep.

A strange noise waked Gordo from his nap. He saw that the golden sunlight had faded from the forest and night was near. Then from a tangled thicket came the cry again, "Cha-cha-lac-a! Cha-cha-lac-a!"

"Now what in the world is that!" exclaimed Gordo as he arched his back.

"Only the six-thirty bird," replied a sleepy-eyed monkey who was curled up in the crotch of the tree.

176

"Why do you call him the six-thirty bird?" asked Gordo.

"The chachalaca is our jungle alarm clock," said the monkey. "His 'cha-cha-lac-a' sounds off at sundown, and the animals who hunt at night know that it is six-thirty and time to go to work. Then again at daylight he sends forth his 'cha-cha-lac-a,' and those of us who hunt during the day know that it is six-thirty—time to get up for breakfast!"

Then Gordo saw the long-tailed chachalaca. It was a dark, gray-brown bird the size of a small hen. It held its head high and called again and again, "Cha-cha-lac-a! Cha-cha-lac-a!"

177

Soon Gordo made his way through the thickets and down to one of the endless marshy swamps. These swamps were picnic grounds for the fat raccoon. Deep in the marshland he found a pale-green lizard and more frogs, crayfish, and duck eggs than his stomach could hold. Farther on, near a fast-moving stream, Gordo saw coatis reaching for fish in the rapids. A wildcat looked down from an overhanging tree. A family of young minks raced up and down the stream and jumped from stone to stone.

Gordo thought of stopping to play along the stream, but suddenly he heard a hoarse coughing sound, "Uh, uh, uh!" He looked and saw what he feared most — a big yellowish-brown cat with rosette-like spots of black! The big animal, weighing two hundred pounds or more, stood with one huge paw lifted. Its lips were drawn back, showing its long, sharp teeth, while it watched the coatis near by.

"El Tigre!" sighed Gordo, as he stealthily crept deep into the marsh.

In the dense marshy growth he heard some-one call, "Where are you? Where are you?" A few feet ahead in his path, Gordo saw a Mexican whippoorwill. The whippoorwill's feathers were mingled gray, brown, and buff. He had stiff whiskers around his large mouth to help him catch insects on the wing at night. Over and over the night bird called, "Par-a-que? Par-a-que?" To Gordo this sounded like, "Where are you? Where are you?"

"I am right here, but I won't be long!" replied Gordo. "I want to find the flamingos tonight."

"The flamingos will be asleep tonight, but you can find them early in the morning. They fish in the inlet down by the coast," replied the strange whippoorwill.

After telling Gordo the safest way to go to the

inlet, the gray bird flapped away, showing clear bands of white on his tail and wings. For some time Gordo could hear his questioning call, "Par-a-que?"

Gordo reached the inlet at dawn and found a fisherman's happy hunting ground there. A long-legged blue heron, with a small snake in its mouth, was wading among the blue water hyacinths. A gay young kingfisher, sitting on a dead limb over the water, cocked its head as it looked for a fish in the blue-green water. Two wild ducks were diving for fish, and a colorful Mexican tree duck stood on a log and looked at the reflection of its pink legs in the water.

Gordo stayed out of sight for a while and watched the birds. Moving farther down the shore, he came to a sandy point of land that reached out into the water. Along the sandy shore he saw hundreds of little mounds a foot or two high. On the mounds and on the shore around them were hundreds of long-legged, bright-red birds.

182

"There are the flamingos! At last I have found them!" Gordo cried.

The little raccoon shuffled along closer and

closer to the birds. When they discovered him, they filled the air with their honking. Like hundreds of tongues of flame the great birds swept out over the water.

The honking of the flamingos sounded very much like the cry of wild geese. They flew with their long necks and their long legs in a straight line. The black feathers on the wing tips of the bright-red birds made each bird in flight look like a flickering flame.

When Gordo recovered from his surprise, he discovered that the mud mounds were the nests of the flamingos. As he moved closer to the nests, he found a dull-white egg in the cuplike top of nearly every nest. In the rapid rise from their nests, some of the birds had rolled the egg off the mound. Gordo stopped to eat one of the eggs that had been broken in the fall from the nest. He was very much surprised to find that the yolk of the egg was blood-red instead of golden as most egg yolks are.

Soon, just as suddenly as the honking flock had left, they returned and settled all around Gordo. The female birds again covered their eggs. The male birds waded about in the blue shore water and scooped up tiny shellfish in their great hooked beaks. Gordo walked up to one big old bird that was standing on one leg and oiling its feathers.

185

"Mr. Flamingo, where did you get such a beautiful red coat?" he asked.

The old flamingo turned his long neck and lowered his head as he said to Gordo, "I am glad you like our red coats. We flamingos are very proud of them. These red feathers are a mark of the courage of the first flamingos on this coast."

"Won't you tell me about the first flamingos?" asked Gordo.

"The first flamingos on this coast had white feathers," the big bird replied, "and they were very proud of their pure white coats.

"One day a terrible volcano began to rumble like thunder. Soon showers of red-hot rocks and rivers of lava covered the country. The animals ran far from the place, but the glowing rocks and the liquid lava followed them.

"All the birds except the flamingos flew away from the terrible heat. The flamingos decided that they must either put out the fire in the volcano or let the whole world burn up.

"They made trip after trip to the sea. They scooped up water in their great bills and flew back to drop it on the volcano and the glowing lava. They even hovered over the great crater to smother the fire below.

"At last the fires were all put out. As the weary flamingos settled on the shore to rest, they looked at each other in astonishment. Their coats were no longer white! They had been turned flame-red

187

by the heat. The tips of their wings and the ends of
their beaks had been burned black as they dipped
through the flames.

"In some places there are still flamingos with

white coats, and some with white coats that have a rosy trimming. But on this coast we flamingos are proud of our flame-red feathers."

"And you should be," replied Gordo. "Your red coats are beautiful."

The flamingos were very friendly with Gordo and even shared their sea food with him. After a time he asked, "Do you know where any treasures are hidden in the jungle?"

"To be sure," replied an old flamingo. "Deep, deep in the jungle there are some huge stone heads. I have heard that near the largest stone head there is an entrance to a cave. In the cave are the oldest and rarest treasures of all!"

"Thank you, thank you!" said Gordo as he turned to go.

With a great flapping of wings, a red cloud of flamingos flew ahead of Gordo and circled over the place where the stone heads lie in the jungle and where the treasure was supposed to be hidden.

CHAPTER 17 · The Enchanted Opal

Gordo hurried toward the spot over which the flamingos had circled. He thought surely he would find the hidden treasure this time, but he had no idea of what really lay ahead of him.

For many days and nights he scrambled through wild banana thickets, tangled jungle forests, and tropical marshlands. Food was always plentiful, but so were dangers. He was torn by poisonous thorns. His sleep was disturbed by the cries of strange jungle birds. More than once he was almost caught by a big, spotted jaguar.

191

One evening Gordo came to a pool deep in the jungle. A royal flycatcher on a limb over the pool raised and lowered its orange and blue topknot. Four brown coatis walked proudly toward the pool. Their long tails, held straight up in the air with the tips curled, looked like question marks. A small band of sleepy-eyed monkeys looked down from a tree and chattered at the sight of the fat little raccoon.

Seeing no spotted jaguars near, Gordo took a good cool drink from the pool. When he looked up, he saw that several giant stone heads lay here and there in the deep jungle growth.

"This must be the place!" he exclaimed. Turning to the coatis, he said, "I am seeking a hidden treasure. Can you tell me where to find the entrance to a cave near one of these giant stone heads?"

The royal flycatcher rapidly raised and lowered his colorful topknot. The monkeys trilled and chattered. The coatis shook their heads and said,

"Don't look for it, Gordo! That Enchanted Opal will bring you bad luck!"

"What enchanted opal?" asked Gordo.

The chattering of the monkeys grew louder as one old pale-faced fellow swung down to the pool. He looked at Gordo and said, "Some say that the Enchanted Opal is in the lost cave. Let me tell you about it!"

"I never heard of an enchanted opal," said Gordo. "Please do tell me about it."

193

The little monkey ran his hands through his fur and began this strange story:

"Many hundreds of years ago this was not a jungle. It was a great kingdom ruled over by a good king. The people were healthy and happy, for they had plenty of everything they wanted. They built great temples to their gods and fine palaces for their king. All went well until the king became proud and selfish. At last, giving no thought to the needs of his people, he took everything for himself.

"A kind old woman, who was one of the king's subjects, lived all alone in a faraway village. This old woman kept a fire burning day and night on a stone hearth at her home. She would never go far from home because she did not want her fire to go out. She wanted no one to know what was hidden under the stone hearth.

"One day while the old woman gathered wood near her home, she found a strange black egg.

" 'It is a pigeon egg,' she told herself, 'but I never saw a black egg before! I shall not eat this one,

194

but I shall keep it for good luck. Perhaps it has some magic charm!'

"One day she took the egg down from the shelf to look at it. It was no longer a dull-black egg! It glistened like glass, and lights danced in it as they did in the fire on her hearth—now green, now red, now gold, now blue!

"The old woman's hand trembled; and she dropped the strange egg on the hearth, breaking it into two pieces. When she looked down, a tiny dwarf was climbing out of the broken egg! The dwarf picked up the two halves of the sparkling egg, pressed them together, and put them into his pocket!

"The woman was glad to have the dwarf live with her. He was good company for her, and, besides, he could help her keep the fire burning. The dwarf liked her very much, too; but as time went on, he wondered why she was so careful to keep the fire burning all the time.

"While the woman was away one morning, the dwarf put out the fire and moved the stone. Under the hearthstone, he saw a round metal disk. He took up the disk and rubbed the dirt from it. It gleamed like gold!

"The dwarf struck the disk with a sharp rock. It rang and echoed with a great noise that sounded throughout the kingdom. The noise was so loud that it caused the trees to bend down and the waves to roll back from the coast.

"The dwarf was afraid. He put the disk back under the hearth and rebuilt the fire over it.

"The woman, knowing what had happened, rushed home. But the dwarf was so afraid that he said he had done nothing and had heard no noise.

"An old legend declared that whenever the hidden golden disk sounded, the king would lose his throne. Now, when the wicked king heard the mighty noise, he knew it was the sound from the golden disk. He sent his soldiers out at once to find who had struck the disk. He thought he might be able to keep his throne if he killed the one who had found and struck the magic disk.

"The soldiers reported to the king that all the

196

people in the kingdom admitted hearing the noise except the dwarf. The dwarf declared that he had heard nothing. The king then knew that it must be the dwarf who had sounded the disk. He ordered the dwarf brought to his palace.

"The dwarf insisted that he knew nothing of a magic disk and had heard no noise. The king then told the dwarf that he would have to be tested to prove whether he had sounded the disk. The dwarf agreed to take any test that the king would also take.

" 'I'll take the test after you,' replied the king, and he ruled that a soldier should break a basketful of coconuts on the dwarf's head, as a test of his truthfulness.

"When the day set for the test arrived, many people came to see it. The dwarf placed his head on a stone. The king's soldier took a heavy hammer and broke the coconuts, one after another, on the dwarf's head.

"When the last coconut was broken, the people saw that the dwarf was not hurt! He stumbled to his feet, shook his head, and said, 'Now it is your turn, King!'

"The king began to object, but the people told him that he must keep his promise. With the blow of the heavy hammer on the first coconut, the king was dead! Then the people declared the dwarf their new king.

"As long as the old woman lived, the dwarf was a very good king. But at last the old woman died, and without her help and good advice the dwarf king fell into wicked ways.

"He let the old fire on the hearthstone go out. Around the old hearth he built the great stone idols whose giant heads you see here now. He built a strange new idol on the palace grounds, too, and ordered all the people to worship it. On the head of the new idol he placed a very fine clay cup in which he kept a strange, gleaming, egg-like object. He called this object the Enchanted Opal.

"Those who looked upon the Enchanted Opal said that the golden-green glow of a jaguar's eyes and specks of fresh red blood flashed inside its smooth, dark surface!

"The dwarf king became very wicked and made his people suffer more and more. At last the suffering people refused to obey his orders and set upon the wicked dwarf with sticks and stones. It is said that he seized the fiery opal and raced out of the city. In the faraway village he stepped upon the old stone hearth and disappeared in a column of smoke as the great gold disk echoed again.

"At the sound of the disk, the whole earth trembled! The great buildings crumbled and fell! Fire swept over the city! The ocean waves rolled in and swept over the entire country! The people were all killed, and the kingdom was destroyed!

"Through the many years the jungle has grown up and covered all, and this little pool has filled the spot where the golden disk was hidden. Some say that the dwarf still sits in a long-lost cave and treasures the Enchanted Opal that caused so much bad luck."

CHAPTER 18 • A Strange Discovery

When the old monkey had finished his story, Gordo was so frightened that the hair stood up on his back. He put both his little black hands over his mouth. When he finally found his voice, he cried, "Oh, me! Can't anyone do anything about this buried kingdom?"

The monkey was climbing back into the tree. He turned toward Gordo and replied, "We are under the spell of the black opal. Until it is brought again into the sunlight, these beautifully hand-carved temples and palaces will lie hidden in the jungle. No one dares to look for the Enchanted Opal, because of the bad luck it brings!"

Gordo decided to leave this jungle wilderness at once and look no more for the hidden treasure. But his curiosity was so great that he stopped to examine one of the huge stone heads near him. He stood beside the head, which was more than seven feet high, and looked up at the carved features.

"I think I'll climb to the top of this old head just to see what I can see," said Gordo, and up he went. As he scrambled over the big stone lips, which were three feet wide, he lost his footing and tumbled to the ground.

"Look, Grandfather! That raccoon is a magician! He has disappeared!" cried a little monkey who had been sitting on top of the great stone head.

All the monkeys began to chatter as they raced away from the spot. A whole flock of curassows and wild turkeys flew from their overhead perches with a roar of wings. A big jaguar and her three spotted kittens walked quietly out of the jungle growth and had the pool to themselves.

203

All this time, poor Gordo was rolling, bumpity-bump, down a long pole ladder. Finally, he landed in a shallow pool of water, forty feet below the surface of the ground. Gordo had fallen into the mouth of an old, old well—grown over by the jungle for years and years!

"Where on earth am I?" cried Gordo, but there was no one to answer his cry. The very stillness worried him. He felt his way through the inky darkness and finally came to a crack in the wall. He squeezed his fat body through the crack, and found himself in a big underground room.

"A cave!" he cried. "Surely this is where the golden treasure is hidden! How lucky I am!"

As Gordo's eyes became used to the darkness, he saw many strange objects. He also saw thousands of bats hanging from the rocks above and around him.

With great curiosity Gordo examined each thing as he came to it. He found beautifully decorated

pottery. There were also wee stone statues, carved in the forms of monkeys, wild turkeys, and other animals. As he was admiring the stone statues, a bat fluttered to the ground a short distance ahead and dodged dizzily around something on the floor of the cave.

When Gordo reached the spot, he found a stack of papers on the floor.

"Can these papers be important?" he thought as he reached for the one on top. When Gordo took hold of the top paper, he found that the whole stack opened like an accordion. Gordo had found one of the oldest books in America! On the pages, folding back and forth like an accordion, were beautifully colored borders and bright pictures of animals, ornaments, and funny little men.

"These may have been important to someone, but they are not very interesting to me," said Gordo, and he continued on his way through the cave.

Soon he found a great stone box in the shape of a jaguar. The stone top had cracked and fallen into the box. Gordo climbed upon the box and looked into it.

"Can these be the treasures that Father Raccoon had in mind?" he asked himself as he gazed at the pile of colorful objects in the box.

Gordo picked up handfuls of bright-green jade beads; a blue jade turtle; and other figures carved from amethyst, turquoise, crystal, and amber. He turned over and over a small gold duck, a chain of alligator teeth set with jade, and a wee gold jaguar's paw.

"I'll take some of these along," said Gordo as he made his way through the dark cave.

Soon the room became smaller. Gordo felt troubled when he realized that he had come into a narrow passage like a hallway. He thought of turning back, but he was no longer sure of his directions. Suddenly he saw pale rays of light ahead of him.

"Light!" he exclaimed. "I suppose that is sunlight drifting through. Perhaps I can get out of here now!"

When Gordo reached the place where the light came in, he found a tree growing. The tree grew from the floor of the cave up and up and through a hole at the ground level. The sunlight came down through the branches to the floor of the cave.

While Gordo was rejoicing that he could see a way out of the cave, he suddenly stopped and exclaimed, "The dwarf!"

There it was—a weird stone figure of a dwarf, sitting near the foot of the tree. On the dwarf's head was a small stone cup, into which the sunlight fell.

"I wonder what is in that cup!" thought Gordo.

He stood on the stone dwarf's lap and looked into the cup. He saw a fiery opal lying in the cup, flashing its rainbows of mysterious colors.

"The Enchanted Opal!" exclaimed Gordo. "The Enchanted Opal!"

Gordo was a little bothered as he thought of the old monkey's story. He recalled, too, that the coatis had said that the opal would bring bad luck.

Undecided, he turned and looked again at the flashing, dark stone. Then he said to himself, "Perhaps they were just teasing me. I'm getting out of this chilly old cave, but I'm taking that Enchanted Opal with me!"

He dropped into the lap of the dwarf the treasures he had brought from the jaguar box. Then he seized the gleaming black opal and scooted up the trunk of the tree.

Gordo soon crawled through the matted vines and stiff orchids on the tree. It was good to be in the sunlight again. A hundred or more yellow and green parrots rose from the treetop and filled the air with their chattering.

Although the sun was high in the sky, Gordo did not go to bed. Since he could never feel comfortable in that jungle now, he decided to travel toward the village.

When Gordo reached the village, he saw tourists coming out of an airplane on a landing field. He watched as they started to the ruins of an old

temple near by. Then he made his way to a little house and hid under the porch.

Gordo was hungry; and when the children who were playing in the yard threw crumbs to him, he crept out from under the porch. Soon he dropped the opal on the ground and began to eat the crumbs.

"Look, a black opal!" cried a little girl. She ran to pick up the opal. This frightened Gordo and he ran away, leaving the opal behind for the little girl.

The empty airplane was standing at the landing field. Gordo climbed into it and hid. He was very tired, and in a little while he was sound asleep. When he waked up, the roaring airplane was winging its way across the country.

The little raccoon would never know that the news of finding the Enchanted Opal would bring many more tourists and much wealth to the country. He would never know that his bringing the opal into the sunlight had broken the spell of the wicked dwarf. He would never know that the beautiful old stone temples would be reclaimed from the jungle and restored for all to see and admire.

CHAPTER 19 · **Wisdom in a Treetop**

The airplane carried Gordo far beyond Mexico City. When it landed, he slipped out into the shadows. He found that he was in a quaint little town with steep, narrow streets. He followed one crooked little street up to the top of a cliff where he could look down upon the old twin-towered church, far below.

Gordo was glad to get away from the big airplane with its noise and its smell of gasoline. He left the town and finally came to an old silver mine.

"The treasure might be here," he thought. But with all his careful searching, he could find no hidden treasure in the deserted mine.

When Gordo came out to the road, he saw a man carrying a big load of wood on his back. Gordo thought if he could get on that load of wood, he could have a good ride. Just then the man stopped to rest. While the man was drinking water from the gourd that he carried, Gordo climbed on top of the load of wood. For hours the man jogged along the road, never knowing that a fat raccoon rode on top of his wood.

"I might catch a good trout here," said Gordo to himself, as the man approached a tropical river.

Soon he jumped off the wood and made his way down to the river. He found a quiet bank and looked out upon the water. As he gazed, several black heads appeared in the water.

"Oh, such big fish! I don't think I could catch one of them!" exclaimed Gordo.

"No, but one of them could catch you," bellowed a deep voice beside Gordo.

Gordo looked just in time to see a big mouth open and a huge alligator slide into the water.

"Alligators! Oh, my!" exclaimed Gordo. "That alligator's mouth looked like the mouth of one of the feathered serpents on the Temple of Quetzalcoatl! I'll not do any fishing in this river!" He hurriedly returned to the road, where he could catch crickets and perhaps a baby bird for lunch.

Before long a burro train, loaded with coconuts from the coast, stopped to rest beside the river. Gordo climbed onto a crate of coconuts and rode for miles when the train moved on again. Every time he looked at the coconuts, he thought how terrible it would be to have one of them cracked on his head!

Little by little Gordo climbed from the hot lands into higher country. One day he found himself on the shore of a very beautiful lake with a pretty green island in it.

"I'd like to go over to that island," thought Gordo.

The little raccoon waded into the blue lake. He

swam until he became tired; then he climbed up on a log and floated along in the sunlight. Finally he jumped back into the water and swam to the shore. On the island, he found a village with steep little streets almost completely curtained with hundreds of big winged nets. Some of the nets were stretched on poles to dry. Others were being mended by the women and the old men of the village.

As Gordo poked his nose under one big net, a shaggy white dog leaped upon him. Dog, raccoon, and net came down in a tangle!

Gordo was a match for any dog his size. He fought furiously, as any good raccoon will when

218

cornered. He rolled over on his back and slashed at the dog with his sharp claws until red streaks appeared in the dog's white hair. Then Gordo jumped up and ran toward the lake. The dog was gaining on him, but any dog knows better than to follow a raccoon into the water. When Gordo entered the water, the shaggy dog stopped on the shore. He knew that a raccoon can hold a dog's head under water until the dog is dead!

When the dog left, Gordo hid in the bottom of a dugout boat that he found tied up at the shore. Soon the owner of the boat returned, got into the boat, and started across the lake. When the boat was well out from shore, the man stood up in his boat and cast out great white nets. The nets looked like giant butterfly wings fastened to a pole. The man scooped up a great pile of slimy, white fish in the nets and poured them into the back of the boat.

"Never have I seen so many fish! Never have I got so much good food with such ease!" laughed Gordo to himself.

When the boat reached the shore, Gordo had eaten all his stomach could hold. He crawled out of the boat and ran into a woodland that was near by. There he climbed into a tree to take a good siesta. The shady grove that Gordo had chosen had also attracted other creatures who joined him there for a siesta.

"Who are you? Where did you come from?" asked an impudent little tree frog as Gordo climbed past him.

"I am Gordo, and I came from far away in the land of flamingos and enchanted opals," replied Gordo.

"How did you get away over here?" asked a sleepy-eyed bat who was hanging from a limb with his wings wrapped tight around his head.

"I flew," bragged Gordo.

"You can't fly! No raccoon can fly!" said Cara-cara, the big black and white hawk in the top of the tree.

"I beg your pardon," replied Gordo, "but I did fly! I flew in a big airplane!"

There was quite a shuffling in the trees and also on the ground. All the animals wanted to see the raccoon who had had such an adventure as a trip in an airplane.

A deer and her twin fawns rose and came near the tree in which Gordo sat. A fox poked his golden-red head out of the underbrush. A big old terrapin thrust his head out from under his protecting shell. An opossum let herself down by the tail so that she could hear what was being said. Caracara rose high in the air and then swooped down to the very limb on which Gordo was resting.

"Tell me about this birdlike airplane. How does

the big thing fly?" asked the black and white hawk.

"I do not know how the airplane flies," Gordo replied. "I only know that it makes a terrible noise and that the smell of the gasoline almost chokes you. But it can fly, day or night, for it can be guided anywhere by the use of something people call radar. You see, people are very wise."

"So people are very wise! Indeed!" squeaked the sleepy-eyed bat. "Now they use radar! Well, let me tell you something, Mr. Raccoon. We bats have used 'radar' for thousands of years. People's radio waves bounce back to warn them of nearby objects, I suppose. Well, all our lives we bats have used sound waves for that same purpose. Bats never bump into things, whether they see them or not. Radar, indeed!"

"Yes, and where do you think people got their
idea for a glider? From us!" chattered a flying
squirrel as he came in for a landing on the limb
below Gordo. "Wise, are they? Well, we flying
squirrels have been gliding through space for
thousands of years!"

"It took people centuries to learn about armored tanks, but we terrapins have always used such things. Not so wise, I'd say," added the old terrapin as he wagged his head from side to side.

"Yes, and we tree frogs had been sticking to trees for ages before people ever thought of using suction cups!" trilled the little green tree frog.

The deer stretched her neck and said, "Think

how long it took people to find out about camouflage! We deer have always used spotted coats on our fawns. El Tigre, even when he is grown, wears a sleek spotted coat. The horned toad wears horns on his pale, sand-colored body. Many birds lay speckled eggs. We animals used the art of camouflage long before people thought about it!"

A big red wasp flipped his wings and said, "People learned from the wasps how to make both paper and clay. Plaster! Adobe! We used them first!"

"Yes, and think how long it took people to discover the value of incubators!" said the opossum. "From the beginning of time every opossum mother has carried a cozy incubator for her tiny babies to snuggle safely in."

Caracara stretched his wings and said, "No, Gordo, people are not so wise. It took them thousands of years to copy the claws of hawks and eagles for their tongs. And you know, we fly without all that noise and that awful smell of gasoline! I wonder if they will ever figure that out!"

By now, Gordo did not know whether people were wise or not. He was quite sure that he was not wise to say that they were.

Before Gordo had time to speak, someone said, "Don't forget that my family had protected itself with gas warfare long before people even knew how to make gas!"

"It is the skunk!" cried the deer as she hustled her two fawns away.

"The skunk! Oh, my!" exclaimed the terrapin as he drew his head, feet, and tail inside his shell.

One by one the animals on the ground crept away, and those in the tree climbed higher and higher. The skunk, fanning his plumy tail over his black and white back, walked slowly toward the lake. Everyone breathed a sigh of relief, and soon all settled down for the afternoon siesta.

CHAPTER 20 • Why Cuckoos Build No Nests

Gordo was ready to continue his journey when he noticed a cuckoo sitting beside him. This was a squirrel cuckoo, a dull-gray bird with eyes as red as rubies.

"Hello, Mr. Cuckoo! I like your bright-red eyes!" said Gordo.

"I like your mask and your black-ringed tail, too," said the cuckoo.

"I have heard that you cuckoos do not build nests—that you lay your eggs in other birds' nests. Is that true, Mr. Cuckoo?" asked Gordo.

"You ought to know, Mr. Raccoon. I hear that

you are quite an authority on birds' nests!" replied the cuckoo. Then he laughed and added, "It is true that most cuckoos build no nests. We were freed from building nests as a reward for some work we did."

"What was the work for which you were rewarded?" asked Gordo.

The cuckoo turned his head from one side to the other, blinked his flaming-red eyes, and told Gordo this story:

"For many years after Quetzalcoatl brought corn to the people of Mexico, the fields were rich and the harvests were good. Finally the soil became so poor that it would not grow enough corn for the people. The people began to complain of being hungry. The harvest gods knew that something must be done.

"They told the people to burn off all the fields and let them rest for a time. Then they could plant the seeds again. But the harvest gods forgot to tell them to save enough seeds for the new planting.

230

"After the fires were started, all the birds were called to a conference. They were asked to fly over the burning fields and gather enough seed corn for the new crop.

"The birds agreed to gather the seeds; but when they saw the flames and felt the heat, they were afraid. All the birds except the cuckoos flew away to the forest without gathering any seeds. The cuckoos stayed and made trip after trip through the fiery cornfields. They saved a big enough supply of seeds to plant the new cornfields.

"The cuckoos' fine feathers were covered with gray ashes, and their eyes were burned until they were the color of the red flames. When the seeds were safely stored, the harvest gods thanked the cuckoos and praised them for being so brave. As a reward for their hard work and their bravery, the cuckoos were told that they would be freed from the task of building nests. From that day to this, they were given the right to lay their eggs in other birds' nests; and that is what many cuckoos do."

Gordo liked the cuckoo's story and thought the cuckoo might help him find the golden treasure. He said to the bird, "I like your story, and I still like those ruby-red eyes. I'd like it a lot if you could tell me where to look for a fine hidden treasure!"

"If you are seeking hidden treasure, I would suggest that you look in a cornfield," said the cuckoo.

"In a cornfield?" asked Gordo, surprised.

"Yes," replied the red-eyed bird. "Go to the old city near here—the place of the hummingbirds. Not far away from this old city is a cornfield where the treasure was hidden long ago."

"What is this treasure? Tell me about it!" exclaimed Gordo.

"It is the treasure of the last king of the people who live here," said the cuckoo. "Just before the Spaniards captured the king, it is said that he melted all the fine gold objects and gems from his palace. He melted his treasures in a great copper

232

pot that only his people knew how to make. Then he plowed a deep furrow in a cornfield and poured the hot liquid gold into the furrow.

"As the good king covered the furrow, he said, 'The Spaniards are greedy for our gold, but they will never find this. Some day when the ground becomes tired and will not grow enough corn for my people, this gold will return to make the soil rich again. Then all the world will come to our door. When they see the beautiful things that my people make, they will pay much gold for them.' "

"Oh, dear me! What became of the great king?" asked Gordo.

The cuckoo continued, "The king returned to his palace. Because he would not tell the Spaniards where to find the gold, alas, he was killed. The Spaniards never found the gold. It still lies where the king buried it, but no one knows exactly where that spot is."

"I think I'll go over that way and see what I can find," said Gordo.

The raccoon said good-by to the friendly cuckoo and then ran joyfully along his way. He passed groves of coffee trees gay with their shiny red berries. At last he came to the old city—the place of the hummingbirds—which is now just a little village.

It was sunset, and Gordo heard a church bell ringing. He thought he had never heard a bell with such a soft, pleasant sound. He turned to a squirrel who was sitting on a stump near by.

"What makes this bell ring so sweetly?" Gordo asked.

"I have heard that it rings more sweetly than other bells because it holds in its throat all the faith of its people and their love for freedom," replied the squirrel. "It seems that the people determined not to let the Spaniards have their treasures. Before the Spaniards got to this city, the people melted all their gold and jewels. From the melted treasures they made this great bell. They think that it still sings of their love of freedom."

"I think it does, too," said Gordo, "and I'm glad that the invaders did not find the people's treasures."

CHAPTER 21 • The Monster in a Cornfield

Gordo crossed several fields where dry corn-stalks lay, but he could find no signs of hidden treasure. When dawn came, he climbed high in an old cedar tree to rest. Soon a man and a boy with two tan-and-white oxen appeared.

Gordo watched the group go to a field with a fence of maguey plants around it and heard the man call, "Arre! Arre!" When the oxen started, Gordo saw that they were pulling a quaint little wooden plow through the rocky soil. The man plowed furrow after furrow. The boy followed, dropping yellow grains of corn into the freshly turned soil.

After a while Gordo saw the boy put his ear to

237

the ground and then call to his father. He saw the man bend down over the furrow and listen.

Gordo turned his head to one side and listened, too. "There is a noise in the ground. I hear it," said Gordo to himself. "It roars louder than a big jaguar! It sounds like thunder under the ground!"

By that time the man was stamping his foot on the ground. Gordo watched and exclaimed, "Smoke! There is a puff of smoke coming from the furrow!"

The man took off his big hat and beat at the spot from which the smoke was rising. But the column of smoke grew bigger. The roaring in the earth grew louder. Flames then shot up into the air with the smoke.

Gordo heard the man cry to his son, "Run, run! The monster is coming up!"

The man and the boy ran from the field, taking their oxen with them. Gordo climbed higher in the cedar tree to see what would happen next. He thought of the fireworks that he had set off in the village. He thought of the flash that he had caused the strange black box to make. He thought of the story of the mad volcano that had given the flamingos their red coats. He was glad that he had done nothing to bring this roaring monster out of the ground.

Soon flames poured forth, and red-hot showers of rocks and ashes fell all over the place. It seemed as if all the rocks locked inside the earth had been loosened and were struggling to come out. People came to look and then, helpless, ran away to safety.

The birds and the squirrels left the neighboring trees. Gordo, also, sought shelter in a tree farther away from the red monster. Liquid lava rolled over the countryside. Red-hot rocks and glowing cinders stripped the nearby trees of their leaves and covered the old cedar and the maguey plants with black ashes and dust.

Within a few hours a mound was formed around the rim of the exploding hole in the cornfield. In a week this mound grew to be a hill. Later the hill grew to be a mountain!

The red flames and smoke, rising high in the air,
seemed to reach for the stars. The glowing lava
ran down in streams that looked like rivers of
melted gold. The rocks whizzed high into the
air and fell with a pounding roar. The red-hot
lava, spreading out over the land, turned to a car-
pet of black rock as it cooled. The ashes piled up
many feet deep and finally became so heavy on

the roofs of houses that the houses tumbled down! And still the roaring, moaning, wailing monster under the earth poured out its streams of liquid lava and showers of glowing rocks and starlike sparks!

Gordo had never dreamed of such fireworks as these. As the days passed and the flow of lava and cloud of ashes had crept on and on, he had retreated farther and farther away. The nearby trees and even the nearest village were almost completely covered now.

Looking about him, Gordo could see people leaving their homes as the glowing flood crept nearer. A giant column of flames flickered and lighted up the night. It made the people look as if they were walking into the sky on stilts of shadows.

"The birds have gone," said Gordo to himself. "The squirrels have gone. The deer and the rabbits have gone. And there goes Mr. Coyote now. I think it is time for me to go, too. I have seen a volcano born in a cornfield!"

242

Gordo took one last look at the fiery monster in the cornfield; then he made his way down the dust-choked road. He thought of the story the cuckoo had told him and wondered if all these rivers of liquid, golden lava could be the king's melted treasure, returning to enrich the soil.

Gordo found that the roads were rough and the broad fields were spoiled. He hardly knew when he passed through the first village, for the clouds of dust and ashes wiped out the walls from his view.

At last he left the worst of the dust behind him and came again to the old town with the wonderful bell—the place of the hummingbirds. The great bell was silent, and Gordo did not stop.

"This time I am going home! No more searching for treasure!" he said, and he traveled steadily on.

CHAPTER 22 • Hidden Treasure

Gordo was eager to get home. He traveled day and night and ate whatever he could find without having to search for it.

He saw a great eagle eating a snake one morning. It made him think of the legend that Eyra had told him of the Mexican flag.

He had to crawl deep into a sticky prickly pear one night to escape from a hungry coyote that was ready to pounce upon him. That made him recall the night he spent under the maguey plant, when the man with the gourd filled the bulging pigskin bag with honey water.

He almost put his hand into a steel trap to get a shiny piece of metal one day. That made him remember the queer old coin and the golden frog that he found in the old wishing well.

These places seemed far away to Gordo now. It was his own safe woodland that he longed to see. He wondered how his mother and father were and what his brother and sisters were doing. He wanted to snuggle down in the cozy hole in his old den tree.

The weather had been warm in the south where Gordo had been, except on the mountains and volcanoes. He had not realized that winter had passed. Now he found that it was warm in northern Mexico, too. Summer had come to his old home. He liked the sounds he heard in the woods— the hum of bees, the chirp of a cricket, the rustle of a bird's wings. As he came nearer home, he became more restless and more eager to get there.

At last one night he found that he was entering the desert country again, this time from the west.

246

The desert was still a desert, however—sand, sand, sand; cactus, cactus, cactus!

"I wish I could find Mr. Jeep," thought Gordo. "He thinks he's so smart! He thinks he has seen and heard everything! How I would like to tell him about red flamingos, enchanted opals, and mad volcanoes!"

"Did you find the hidden treasure?" asked a voice behind him.

Poor Gordo was so surprised to see Mr. Jeep that he stopped with his mouth open.

"Did you? Did you find the hidden treasure?"
asked Mr. Jeep again.

"No," replied Gordo.

"You didn't? In all this time you didn't find the
treasure?" asked Mr. Jeep.

Gordo thought to himself, "Perhaps I am not so
smart either. After all I didn't find that treasure.

And why should I bother to tell Mr. Jeep about the things I saw? He wouldn't believe it. And besides I am in a hurry to get home." Then he laughed and said to Mr. Jeep, "No—didn't find it. I'm on my way home now."

"Too bad," said jolly Mr. Jeep. "But do look at my desert before you go. It is beautiful when it is in bloom."

Gordo looked all around and exclaimed, "Oh, Mr. Jeep, it is beautiful!"

One spreading cactus looked like a bunch of flaming torches, for each long arm was tipped with a cluster of bright-red flowers. Around the top of the barrel cactus was a great crown of greenish yellow blooms. The thorny prickly pears were decorated with satiny rose and gold. Creamy-white flowers filled the tips of every branch and spilled over to bloom down the sides of the giant stalk where the elf owl made his home. The sprawling creosote bush was weighed down with silken gold. As if lighting the desert for all to enjoy, the yuccas had sent up from their gray-green spikes tall stems of waxy blossoms that gleamed like white candles in the night.

As Gordo looked around, he thought of his first night on the desert—of the galloping ghost, of the elf owl, and of Mr. White-throat and his second-hand store. Then he turned to Mr. Jeep and said, "Yes, Mr. Jeep, your desert is beautiful tonight. I wish I could stay longer, but I must be going now. You see, I want to get home tonight."

Gordo said good-by to Mr. Jeep and hurried along his way. After a while he heard bells ringing—the same bells that he had heard in the village the night he left home. As he listened he said, "The bells are ringing for the early service. Daylight will come soon."

Gordo remembered the trouble he had had in villages before—being hunted by people with sticks and stones, being shut up in a box, being spurred by a fighting cock!

He said to himself, "I'll not go through the village with the singing bells. I'll cut across this field to my woodland home."

Gordo found tall plants growing in the field. He noticed that they made a rustling sound in the wind. He stopped and examined one of the plants.

"Why, this is corn!" he exclaimed. "I have never seen big corn plants like these before!"

The fat raccoon, who was a big, grown-up fellow now, stood on his hind legs and felt of one of the hard bundles that were growing on the cornstalk. He pulled at the green wrapping on the bundle and finally stripped it off. He stared for a moment at the rich golden grains of corn. They almost sparkled in the moonlight.

Gordo held the ear of corn in his hands and bit into the golden grains. Then he greedily nibbled down the ear to the very end of it.

"Yum, yum, yum!" he cried as the sweet, milky juice spattered over his black mask. "This is the best thing I have ever tasted! This is a real golden treasure!"

Then, as he stripped the shucks from another ear of corn, he suddenly exclaimed, "This is it! Of course it is! This is the hidden golden treasure that Father had in mind! It is the finest treasure in the world!"

There was a rustling among the cornstalks. Gordo looked up and saw five big raccoons pulling off golden ears of corn. He heard the biggest raccoon say, "Eat all you want. It is just right for eating tonight. How I wish Gordo could be here to enjoy it, too."

Then Gordo knew that the raccoons were his own family. There were his father and his mother! There were his sisters and brother, who were almost as large now as their parents! Gordo's happiness rang in his voice as he called, "Mother, Father! I am Gordo! Don't you know me?"

"Gordo! Gordo!" cried the mother and the father raccoon in one breath. "Oh, how glad I am that you are home again!" cried Gordo's mother.

254

"You have found the hidden treasure!" said Gordo's father proudly.

"Yes," laughed Gordo, "and it is the very best treasure in the world!"

"Fresh, golden corn, milky and sweet, hidden in clean green shucks, is truly the finest treasure in the world for raccoons," agreed the old raccoon.

"But where have you been?" asked Gordo's

255

mother. "We thought that a hungry coyote must have caught you!"

"I went to look for this hidden treasure," replied Gordo. "All over Mexico I have looked for it. But I had to come home to find it—right here under my nose, as Rojo said it might be!"

"All over Mexico!" said one young raccoon.

"What did you see? What did you find?" asked the other two.

"Many and strange things!" said Gordo.

The first streaks of light were showing in the east as the happy raccoon family walked home together to their old den tree.

At the foot of the tree they sat and listened in amazement as Gordo told them of desert ghosts, of ancient pyramids, of floating gardens, of ruins in the jungle, of legends told by the Aztecs, and of the terrible fiery monster that exploded in a cornfield.

Glossary

Key to Pronunciation

This Glossary will help you to pronounce some of the words you may not know. It will also give you the definitions of these words unless the meaning is explained where the word appears in the book. The meaning given for a word will help you to understand the word as it is used in this book.

The respellings in parentheses after word entries and the pronunciation key will help you in pronouncing words. Notice all diacritical marks. These marks will help you to get the proper sounds in syllables. Watch the accent marks. The primary, or heavy, accent mark (′) is placed after a syllable that has a strong accent, or voice stress. The lighter accent mark (′) shows a secondary, or lighter, accent.

ā as in āte	ĕ as in silĕnt	o͝o as in fo͝ot
å as in våcation	ē̃ as in watē̃r	
ă as in ăt		ū as in cūbe
ă as in *ă*ccount	ī as in īce	u̇ as in u̇nite
ä as in ärm	ĭ as in hĭt	ŭ as in ŭp
ȧ as in ȧsk		*ŭ* as in circ*ŭ*s
a as in sof*a*	ō as in gō	û as in hûrt
â as in câre	ȯ as in ȯbey	
	ŏ as in tŏp	th (thick sound) as
ē as in bē	*ŏ* as in *ŏ*ccur	in feather
ė as in ėvent	ô as in ôrb	th (thin sound) as
ĕ as in gĕt	o͞o as in mo͞on	in thin

The definitions and diacritical markings are based upon *Webster's New International Dictionary.*

Glossary

A

accordion (ă-kôr′dĭ-ŭn), a small wind instrument; creased or hinged so as to fold like an accordion.

adobe (à-dō′bĭ), an unburnt brick dried in the sun; clay from which unburnt bricks are made.

ahuehuete (ä-wȧ-wā′tȧ), a giant cypress tree found in Mexico.

Ahuehuetzin (ä′wȧ-wāt′sĭn).

amber (ăm′bēr), a reddish-yellow resin somewhat like the sap of pine trees after it has hardened. It takes a fine polish and is used for jewelry.

amethyst (ăm′ė-thĭst), a clear purple or bluish-violet variety of crystallized quartz.

amigo (ä-mē′gō), a friend; a Spanish term applied to friendly natives.

ancient (ān′shĕnt), very old; one who lived long ago.

armadillo (är′mȧ-dĭl′ō), a burrowing mammal with an upper covering of bony plates or scales.

armor (är′mēr), protective covering for a body in battle.

Arre! (är′rȧ), the Spanish word for "Get up!"—used by drivers of horses, donkeys, and mules.

authority (ô-thŏr′ĭ-tĭ), a right to command or to act.

avocado (ăv-ô-kä′dō), a tree bearing pearlike fruit eaten as a salad; the fruit is also called alligator pear.

Aztecs (ăz′tĕks), the Indians that founded and developed the Mexican empire.

B

balcony (băl′kō-nĭ), a platform pro- jecting from the wall of a building, enclosed by a railing.

bamboo (băm-bōō′), a canelike grass.

banderilla (bän-dȧ-rēl′yä), a barbed dart.

buff-colored (bŭf′kŭl′ērd), a pale or faded yellowish-orange color.

burro (bûr′ō), a donkey, especially a small one used as a pack animal.

C

calculating (kăl′kū-lāt′ĭng), figuring; finding out and fixing by rules of arithmetic.

calendar (kăl′ĕn-dēr), an orderly arrangement of the divisions of time, as years, months, weeks, days.

camouflage (kăm′ōō-fläzh), hiding by disguising.

capital (kăp′ĭ-tăl), a chief city; the seat of government.

caracara (kä′rȧ-kä′rȧ), a large hawk.

carnation (kär-nā′shŭn), any of the cultivated varieties of the clove pink; a double-flowered pink.

carved (kärvd), cut in an artistic way; made, shaped, or formed by cutting.

cast (kȧst), to throw or fling with a quick motion.

century (sĕn′tū-rĭ), a period of one hundred years.

Cha-cha (chä′chä).

chachalaca (chä′chȧ-lä′kȧ).

circular (sûr′kū-lēr), round; ring-shaped.

clacking (klăk′ĭng), making abrupt clattering sounds rapidly.

coati (kô-ä′tė), a raccoon-like animal of tropical America.

cobblestone (kŏb″l-stōn′), a rounded stone used for paving.

259

column (kŏl'ŭm), an upright body or mass; a pillar.

commotion (kŏ-mō'shŭn), disorder; disturbance.

copper (kŏp'ēr), a common metal of a reddish-brown color.

coral (kŏr'ăl), the skeletons of very small sea animals, used for jewelry and ornaments, often red in color.

costume (kŏs'tūm), distinctive dress or suit worn by people in a locality, or for special occasions.

courage (kûr'ĭj), that spirit of mind that helps one to meet danger with firmness.

crater (krā'tēr), the cup- or saucer-shaped opening, or mouth, of a volcano.

creosote (krē'ŏ-sōt), a desert shrub found in the southwestern United States and northern Mexico.

crotch (krŏch), a separation into trunk and branch, or into two branches of a tree; a fork.

crunching (krŭnch'ĭng), a grinding or crushing; a noise made by crushing or biting.

crystal (krĭs'tăl), a clear, brilliant hard glass.

cuckoo (kŏŏk'ōō), a large grayish-brown bird that lays its eggs in nests of other birds.

curiosity (kū'rĭ-ŏs'ĭ-tĭ), wanting to inquire into anything; meddlesomeness; an object valued for rarity or strangeness.

curassow (kū'rȧ-sō).

cypress (sī'prĭs), a timber tree, usually evergreen, somewhat resembling a large cedar.

D

dense (dĕns), crowded together; close; thick.

disk (dĭsk), a round, flat, platelike object.

dough (dō), a soft mass of moistened flour or meal thick enough to roll.

dwarf (dwôrf), an animal or plant much below the normal size of its kind.

dye (dī), color; to stain, to color.

E

echo (ĕk'ō), the repetition of a sound by reflection of sound waves.

El Capitán (ĕl kä'pē-tän'), the captain.

elf (ĕlf), a fairy; a small, lively, mischievous child or animal.

El Tigre (ĕl tē'grả).

emblem (ĕm'blĕm), a sign or picture that stands for another object or idea.

enchant (ĕn-chȧnt'), to charm, as by a witch's spell.

Eyra (ā'rȧ).

F

faith (fāth), belief in God; complete confidence.

familiar (fȧ-mĭl'yēr), well known; common.

fascinated (făs'ĭ-nāt'ĕd), held by; captivated or charmed by.

fiber (fī'bēr), slender, threadlike tissue.

fiercest (fēr'sĕst), most savage; most cruel.

fiery (fī'rĭ), bearing fire; glowing; resembling fire.

fiesta (fyĕs'tä), a holiday; a feast; a religious festival.

Flaco (fläk'ồ).

flamingo (flȧ-mĭng'gō), an American waterbird with long legs and neck, webbed feet, and bright red plumage.

flirting (flûrt'ĭng), to open or close briskly.

fountain (foun'tĭn), a spring; a source.

fragrance (frā'grăns), a sweet smell; perfume.

furrow (fûr'ō), a trench.

G

gardenia (gär-dē'nĭ-à), a cape jasmine; a plant having showy, fragrant white blossoms.

gazed (gāzd), looked at steadily; stared at.

gem (jĕm), a precious stone; something prized for great beauty or great worth.

geranium (jē-rā'nĭ-ŭm), a plant bearing clusters of bright flowers, often orange-red in color.

gleam (glēm), a glow; a flash of brightness.

goblin (gŏb'lĭn), an evil, misshapen sprite, believed to live in the woods.

gopher (gō'fēr), a burrowing rodent the size of a large rat; a small ground squirrel, much like a chipmunk.

Gordo (gôr'dȯ), a Spanish word meaning fat, plump, full-fed.

grackle (grăk''l), a large black bird having glossy and iridescent plumage.

grief (grēf), sadness.

grove (grōv), a smaller group of trees than a forest, and without underbrush.

guitar (gĭ-tär'), a stringed musical instrument with a long fretted neck and six strings.

H

hearth (härth), the floor of a fireplace; a stone on which a fire is burned.

heron (hĕr'ŭn), a wading waterbird that feeds upon fish and other small water animals which it catches by a quick jab of its long bill.

Hidalgo (ē-däl'gȯ).

hover (hŭv'ēr), to hang fluttering in the air; to move to and fro over or about a place.

hurl (hûrl), to fling, to throw violently.

hustled (hŭs''ld), moved quickly; pushed out of the place.

hyacinth (hī'à-sĭnth), a flowering plant having spikes of bell-shaped flowers—blue, pink, purple, or yellow.

I

idol (ī'dŭl), an image of a god used as an object of worship.

incubator (ĭn'kŭ-bā'tēr), a place for raising premature babies; a machine by which eggs are hatched artificially.

indicates (ĭn'dĭ-kāts), points out or to; shows; states.

insist (ĭn-sĭst'), to take a stand and refuse to give way.

invade (ĭn-vād'), to enter with intention to conquer.

investigate (ĭn-vĕs'tĭ-gāt), to follow up; to examine.

Ixta (ēs'tä).

Ixtacíhuatl (ēs'tä-sē'wä-t'l).

J

jade (jād), a gem stone, commonly green in color.

jaguar (jăg'wär), a fierce forest cat, resembling the leopard.

javelina (hä'vĕ-lē'nä), a wild hog; a peccary in Mexico and Texas.

jewels (jōō'ĕls), costly ornaments of gold, silver, or the like; cut stones polished for use as ornaments.

jogged (jŏgd), moved at a slow pace.

K

kangaroo (kăng'gà-rōō'), a leaping marsupial mammal of Australia.

261

L

lacking (lăk′ĭng), to be without; to be needing.

lava (lä′và), fluid rock which flows from volcanoes.

legend (lĕj′ĕnd), a story of miracles or wonders handed down from the past.

M

macaw (mà-kô′), a large, long-tailed parrot found in South and Central America.

maguey (măg′wā), the century plant, valued for its fibers. It is valued also for the sap which flows when the leaves are cut.

Manito (mä-nē′tô).

María (mä-rē′á).

masked (màskt), covered; concealed.

Mayan (mä′yăn), an Indian of the Mayas; belonging to the Mayas.

mesquite (mĕs-kēt′), a thorny, deep-rooted tree or shrub found in the southwestern United States and Mexico.

Mexican (mĕk′sĭ-kăn), a native of Mexico; of Mexico or its people.

Mexico (mĕk′sê-kō), a republic lying to the south of the United States.

midst (mĭdst), the middle.

mingle (mĭng′g'l), to put together; to mix.

mischievous (mĭs′chĭ-vŭs), full of mischief; injurious; harmful.

mumbled (mŭm′b'ld), spoken indistinctly.

museum (mû-zē′ŭm), a building or place in which are kept objects of permanent interest.

mussel (mŭs″l), fresh-water, bivalve mollusk.

N

national (năsh′ŭn-ăl), peculiar to a particular nation, as the *national* song of a country.

native (nā′tĭv), born in or belonging to a particular country or place.

Negrito (nê-grē′tō).

nimble (nĭm′b'l), moving easily; swift.

O

odd (ŏd), not paired with another; different from what is usual.

oompa (ōŏmp′á).

opal (ō′păl), a mineral; a gem having a peculiar play of colors of delicate tints.

orchid (ôr′kĭd), a tropical "air" plant which bears flowers of rare beauty; a blue-red color.

outwit (out-wĭt′), to outdo in cunning; to be smarter than.

P

palace (păl′ĭs), a large and stately house; the official home of a king; a large public building.

Papán (pä-pän′).

par-a-que (pâr′á′kū).

patio (pä′tĭ-ō), a courtyard within a house or other building, sometimes with a garden in it.

peccary (pĕk′á-rĭ), a javelina; a night-feeding wild pig.

Pedro (pā′drō).

piñatas (pēn-yä′tàs).

plaza (plä′zà), the square or market place; a park.

plodding (plŏd′ĭng), moving or traveling slowly; walking heavily.

pluck (plŭk), to pull off, out, or up; to pick or gather.

Popo (pō′pô).

Popocatépetl (pô-pō′kä-tä′pĕt′l).

262

pulp (pŭlp), soft fleshy part of the fruit.

puma (pū′ma̤), a large member of the cat family; a mountain lion found in the Americas; the cougar.

pyramid (pĭr′a̤-mĭd), a great structure with four triangular faces meeting at a point.

Q

quaint (kwānt), strange but pleasing.

Quetzalcoatl (ket-säl′kȯ-ä′t'l).

R

radar (rā′där), a device for detecting the presence and location of objects by radio waves.

ramble (răm′b'l), to walk from place to place without any purpose; to roam; to wander.

rare (râr), unusual; uncommon; seldom met with or seen.

relic (rĕl′ĭk), that which remains; an object valued because of its association with a saint or a god.

resin (rĕz′ĭn), the dried sap from certain plants and trees.

retreat (rė-trēt′), an act of withdrawing from danger or that which is difficult.

reward (rė-wôrd′), to pay for a service; to make a return for good or evil done.

Rojo (rō′hō).

rosette (rō-zĕt′), like a rose in shape.

royal (roi′a̤l), kingly; belonging to the king; connected with a king's government.

rudder (rŭd′ẽr), that part of a boat that guides or steers it; to act as a guide or governor.

S

Saint (sānt), a holy or godly person.

saucy (sô′sĭ), pert, impudent.

scuttle (skŭt′l), to hasten or hurry.

Señor (så-nyȯr′), a Spanish title of courtesy, as *Mr.* or *sir* in English.

sensitive (sĕn′sĭ-tĭv), having sense or feeling; being quick to react to external sensations.

serpent (sûr′pĕnt), a snake.

shallow (shăl′ō), not deep.

shucks (shŭks), the outer covering of Indian corn, or of nuts such as the peanut or hickory nut.

shuffle (shŭf′l), to move awkwardly; to move with a dragging of thè feet.

siesta (sĭ-ĕs′ta̤), a short sleep or rest, especially at midday.

skeleton (skĕl′ė-tŭn), the bones of a human body; the framework of a thing.

slinky (slĭngk′ĭ), long, thin; gracefully slender.

smoldering (smōl′dẽr-ĭng), smoking.

solemn (sŏl′ĕm), gloomy; highly serious.

sought (sôt), hunted; looked for.

source (sōrs), that from which anything originates.

Spaniard (spăn′yẽrd), a native of Spain or a member of the Spanish race.

spiny (spīn′ĭ), thorny; prickly.

sprawl (sprôl), to lie with body and limbs stretched out.

statue (stăt′ū̇), the likeness of a living thing modeled in clay, stone, or some other solid substance.

stealthy (stĕl′thĭ), sly; furtive.

stilts (stĭlts), poles of wood used to raise the feet above the ground in walking.

stowed (stōd), packed; stored; hid away.

suction (sŭk′shŭn), act or process of

263

sucking; as, holding in place by suction.

syrup (sĭr'ŭp), a thick solution of sugar with juices.

T

tapestry (tăp'ĕs-trĭ), a hand-woven textile, commonly figured, and often used as a wall hanging.

tarantula (tà-răn'tú̇-là), a large spider.

temple (tĕm'p'l), a building for worship; a church building.

thatched (thăcht), having a covering for the roof of grasses, straw, or leaves.

throne (thrōn), a royal seat; a chair of state.

tile (tīl), a piece of fired clay, stone, or the like, used for covering roofs or for floors, walls, etc., of buildings.

tolling (tōl'ĭng), pulling a bell so as to sound the time or a call to worship.

tongs (tŏngs), instruments, usually two-pronged, for taking hold of or handling something.

tortilla (tôr-tē'yä), a round, thin corncake, baked on a hot stone, made especially by the Mexicans.

tower (tou'ĕr), a high building or a high part of a building.

trellis (trĕl'ĭs), a frame of latticework used as a support for climbing plants.

triangular (trī-ăng'gū-lĕr), having three sides.

tropical (trŏp'ĭ-kăl), within the tropics; of the tropics.

tuft (tŭft), a knot or bunch of slender parts held together at one end; a cluster; as, a *tuft* of wool, a *tuft* of grass, a *tuft* of feathers.

twang (twăng), a harsh, quick ringing sound.

turquoise (tûr'kois), a bluish-green, blue, or greenish-gray stone used for ornaments and in jewelry.

V

valuable (văl'ū-à-b'l), highly useful; having the value of money.

ventriloquist (vĕn-trĭl'ō-kwĭst), one who can speak in such a way that the voice seems to come from some other source than the speaker.

volcano (vŏl-kā'nō), an opening in the earth's surface from which molten or hot rock, steam, etc., are thrown out.

W

waddle (wŏd''l), to walk with short steps, swaying from side to side, like a duck.

wand (wŏnd).

weary (wēr'ĭ), tired; worn out in strength.

weird (wērd), strange; odd; unearthly.

wisdom (wĭz'dŭm), knowledge, with the ability to make use of it.

wisp (wĭsp), a small amount.

worship (wûr'shĭp), to show love and faith in God; to respect; to honor.

X

Xochimilco (hō'chê-mēl'kō).

Y

yolk (yōk), the yellow mass of food surrounded by the white in the egg of a bird or reptile.

yonder (yŏn'dĕr), at or in that place; farther; more distant.

yucca (yŭk'à), a plant having long-pointed, stiff leaves and bearing a tall spike of white florets.